PRIZE SURPRISE SWEEPSTAKES!

This month's prize:

A FABULOUS SHARP VIEWCAM!

This month, as a special surprise, we're giving away a Sharp ViewCam**, the big-screen camcorder that has revolutionized home videos!

This is the camcorder everyone's talking about! Sharp's new ViewCam has a big 3" full-color viewing screen with 180° swivel action that lets you control everything you record—and watch it at the same time! Features include a remote control (so you can get into the picture yourself), 8 power zoom, full-range auto focus, battery pack, recharger and more!

The next page contains two Entry Coupons (as does every book you received this shipment). Complete and return *all* the entry coupons; **the more times you enter, the better your chances of winning!**

Then keep your fingers crossed, because you'll find out by November 15, 1995 if you're the winner!

Remember: The more times you enter, the better your chances of winning!*

*NO PURCHASE OR OBLIGATION TO CONTINUE BEING A SUBSCRIBER NECESSARY TO ENTER. SEE THE BACK PAGE FOR ALTERNATE MEANS OF ENTRY, AND RULES.

**THE PROPRIETORS OF THE TRADEMARK ARE NOT ASSOCIATED WITH THIS PROMOTION.

PVC KAL

PRIZE SURPRISE
SWEEPSTAKES

OFFICIAL ENTRY COUPON

This entry must be received by: OCTOBER 30, 1995
This month's winner will be notified by: NOVEMBER 15, 1995

YES, I want to win the Sharp ViewCam! Please enter me in the drawing and let me know if I've won!

Name_____

Address _____ Apt. _____

City   State/Prov.   Zip/Postal Code

Account #_____

Return entry with invoice in reply envelope.

© 1995 HARLEQUIN ENTERPRISES LTD.   CVC KAL

"*I'm not interested in marrying again.*"

Kate continued. "I don't want any husband."

"Interesting," Damon said. He looked at her assessingly for a moment, then smiled grimly. "Sit down, Kate McKee. We have things to talk about."

"What things?"

"I'm a businessman, Ms. McKee. If I can help you and help myself at the same time, I think that's good business."

Kate couldn't imagine any sort of dealings the two of them might conduct that would be mutually beneficial. But then, he was the business tycoon, not her.

"What did you have in mind?"

"I want you to marry me!"

ANNE McALLISTER was born in California. She spent long lazy summers daydreaming on local beaches and studying surfers, swimmers and volleyball players in an effort to find the perfect hero. She finally did, not on the beach, but in a university library where she was working. She, her husband and their four children have since moved to the Midwest. She taught, copyedited, capped deodorant bottles and ghostwrote sermons before turning to her first love, writing romance fiction.

Books by Anne McAllister

Don't miss any of our special offers. Write to us at the following address for information on our newest releases.

Harlequin Reader Service
U.S.: 3010 Walden Ave., P.O. Box 1325, Buffalo, NY 14269
Canadian: P.O. Box 609, Fort Erie, Ont. L2A 5X3

ANNE McALLISTER

The Alexakis Bride

Harlequin Books

TORONTO • NEW YORK • LONDON
AMSTERDAM • PARIS • SYDNEY • HAMBURG
STOCKHOLM • ATHENS • TOKYO • MILAN
MADRID • WARSAW • BUDAPEST • AUCKLAND

ISBN 0-373-11769-8

THE ALEXAKIS BRIDE

First North American Publication 1995.

CHAPTER ONE

'A MAN can never have too many women.'

Damon Alexakis could remember his father saying that as far back as he was able to recall. The old man's rich baritone practically caressed the words as he said them. And then he would look at his only son and give him a conspiratorial wink.

At the ripe old age of thirty-four, when a single man in possession of all the right instincts might most likely have been expected to concur wholeheartedly, Damon Alexakis begged to differ.

It wasn't that he didn't like women. He did. The sort he could take to dinner, take to bed, and forget about the next morning.

It was the other women who were the bane of his existence — the women Aristotle Alexakis had most adored.

But then Aristotle had never been surrounded by and responsible for a widowed mother and six — count them, *six* — hellish sisters. Not to mention five-year-old twin nieces.

The old man had died when Damon was only eighteen, while the girls were still charming everyone in sight. His father, Damon often thought grimly, didn't know what he'd missed.

Now, as Damon drummed his pen on the top of his broad teak desk, then stared distractedly out the window at the midtown New York skyline, he wished, not for the first time, that he were an orphaned only child.

He could have done without them all — without his

5

mother, who was trying to settle him down and provide him with the Perfect Alexakis Bride, without Pandora who had lately dashed off with a shifty Las Vegas blackjack dealer, without Electra who was shedding her clothes in that off-colour, off-off-off Broadway production in the name of art, without Chloe who had taken off for darkest Africa without a word, without Daphne who'd bought all those chinchillas on the hoof because she was sorry for them and not because they'd make lovely coats, without Arete who just this morning had stalked into his office and quit to take a job with Strahan Brothers, Importers, his biggest competitors, and most especially, at the moment, without his eldest sister, Sophia, whose pregnancy was at present complicating his life.

Why, Damon lifted his eyes and asked the heavens, should any man have to worry about his sister's pregnancy? Why shouldn't it be her husband's problem?

Because, he answered on behalf of the heavens, her husband, Stephanos, *was* the problem.

He and Kate McKee.

Kate McKee.

The woman even sounded like trouble. A fiery and frolicsome Titian-haired temptress — exactly the sort of woman that his philandering brother-in-law would be eager to take to bed.

Had no doubt already taken to bed, Damon reminded himself savagely, stabbing his pen into the desk blotter.

All those other mother's helpers Stephanos had hired — Stacy and Tracy and Casey and whoever else had come and gone keeping an eye on his and Sophia's impish twins in the last two months — had been mere red herrings.

It was Kate McKee whom Stephanos had been

intent on installing in his and Sophia's Park Avenue apartment. And in his bed.

Damon knew he should have been suspicious from the moment Stephanos had announced that the doctor recommended a nanny. His brother-in-law was never eager to lay out a penny more than necessary, much less voluntarily pay someone to help not him but his wife.

But Stephanos had been all soulful eyes and deep concern when he'd come into Damon's office that afternoon two months ago. 'The doctor is worried about Sophia. He says she's in danger of miscarrying. She needs someone to keep an eye on the twins.'

'I'll take care of it,' Damon had promised, phone against his ear. He scratched Sophia's name on a pad at the same time he was trying to catch the particulars on a crystal shipment due from Venice that afternoon.

But Stephanos had given Damon an airy wave of his hand. 'It's not your problem. I'm just telling you. I'll interview the girls myself.'

Damon ground his teeth now. He should have known better. Everything that even vaguely affected the lives of any of the Alexakis women ended up being his problem sooner or later!

Kate McKee.

What the hell was he going to do about her?

Fire her tail. That was what he'd like to do. He'd like to drop-kick her from here to Siberia, and send his miserable brother-in-law spiralling the South Pole while he was at it.

He couldn't.

Because Sophia, heaven help him, adored her dear Miss Kate!

'She's such a competent person. So clever. So cheerful. And she takes such good care of the girls. You can't know what a relief it is. Knowing Kate's in charge makes me feel so much better.' Sophia had said all that to him just this morning.

She'd said other equally enthusiastic things about her husband's mistress in the past two weeks. But then Damon hadn't realised what Stephanos was up to.

Now he knew. He'd heard the rumours like everyone else. Except so far, thank God, Sophia. He was going to make sure she never heard them.

And he'd have loved to deal with both Stephanos and his lady love in the way they so richly deserved, except——

'The doctor says I'm doing much better since Kate came,' Sophia had gone on to say. 'She makes all the difference. I don't know what I'd do without Kate.'

So his hands were tied. For the moment at least.

But that didn't mean he was going to tolerate such underhanded goings-on. There was no way he was going to stand by and watch his brother-in-law make a fool of Sophia.

His hands clenched into fists as he contemplated what he'd like to do to Stephanos. Would the competent Miss McKee find her lover quite so attractive with his face rearranged?

But again, he couldn't do that.

Because Sophia would find out.

And now, of all times, the high-strung Sophia needed shielding.

No, he couldn't shift Stephanos's nose for him, and he couldn't blacken his eyes. But he could do a little bit of rearranging.

And Damon intended to start with Kate McKee's expectations!

The phone buzzed. He picked it up, cradling it against his shoulder. 'I thought you'd gone home,' he said to Lilian, his secretary.

'I live here,' Lilian said drily. 'We both do.'

'It seems like it,' Damon admitted. 'What's up?'

'Your mother. On line two.'

'Now?' He glanced at his watch, frowning. 'It's almost two in the morning in Athens.' He sighed. 'All right. Put her through.'

He wondered what disaster had befallen Helena Alexakis this time. His mother was the original clinging vine, a woman who counted on her man to solve everything. And since her husband had died, she never made a move without discussing it with her son. Except, Damon thought grimly, in the case of her search for his perfect bride.

'Damon? Is that you, my son? You are not home? You are still working?'

'Yes, Mama, I'm still working. What's wrong?'

'Nothing. Not one little thing.' He could hear her good cheer even above the transatlantic crackle on the line. 'I'm calling to tell you the good news.'

Damon straightened up, flexing his shoulders, smiling, too, relieved that for once there was no problem. 'Good news, Mama? What's that?'

'I am coming to New York.' A dramatic pause. 'And I am bringing Marina.'

'Your brother wants to meet me?' Kate stopped paring the apple she held in her hand and looked at her employer a bit dubiously.

'This afternoon at three,' Sophia agreed, lounging complacently on the sofa, her knitting untouched in her lap while she watched Kate prepare the twins' lunch.

Kate shook her head. From everything she'd heard about hard-driving, arrogant Damon Alexakis during the three weeks she'd worked for his sister, he didn't seem the sort to waste his precious time on a mother's helper. Even if the mother's helper in question actually owned Kid Kare, Inc. and didn't just work for it.

Unless, she thought with a hint of amusement, he wanted to buy in and start exporting nannies. She supposed, given his penchant for buying and selling, it might be possible. She almost wished it were. Heaven knew it would give credibility to her business's vitality.

'Why would he want to meet me?'

'Damon likes to know everyone involved with the family. It's his way,' Sophia said. 'He feels responsible.'

'Not for me. I'm responsible for myself.'

'Of course. I admire your independence,' Sophia said wistfully. 'I could never be like you. But Damon is a bit old-fashioned, and it's important to humour him. You don't mind, do you?'

'No, of course not.' Kate was aware of the fragility of Sophia's temperament. She had learned quickly not to do or say anything that would make Sophia worry needlessly. She gave the older woman a quick smile. 'I'll be delighted to meet him.'

It would be a chance to tell him a few home truths, she thought. Like what a philandering jerk his brother-in-law was.

If she hadn't known she'd be leaving Sophia in the lurch at a dangerous time, Kate would have left in the middle of the second week, the second she'd escaped from Stephanos's marauding hands and mouth the night he had cornered her in the kitchen. She'd hoped a bit of cold-shoulder treatment would solve the problem. But from the way he was watching her, almost leering whenever Sophia's back was turned, she feared he was biding his time.

If Damon Alexakis was the superman everyone seemed to think he was, maybe he could put a stop to Stephanos's lechery before Kate stopped it herself with a well-placed knee which would cost him some pain, her some embarrassment, and Sophia the woman she needed to keep the twins under control.

Kate wasn't quite sure how she was going to tell Damon Alexakis that, however. She was still mulling it over when the taxi let her off outside the midtown building where Alexakis Enterprises had its offices.

The building was forty storeys — marble and glass. Very sleek and modern-looking, exuding a sort of wealthy energy that reminded Kate all too much of the building four blocks north where her father had his own corporate headquarters.

It made her own tiny office in a converted floor-through brownstone apartment from the mid-seventies seem a store-front venture indeed. She'd certainly been pipe-dreaming when she'd thought he might be interested in it. Damon Alexakis would never be concerned with a small potatoes business like hers!

No, Sophia had to be right. He only wanted to look her over, make sure that Kate McKee wasn't the sort of Irish serving girl whose backward ways and bog-bred brogue might corrupt his precious nieces!

Well, she had no fears of facing him about that.

Lifting her chin and smoothing her hair as best she could, Kate marched into the lift and punched the button for the twentieth floor.

'Mr Alexakis is expecting you,' the secretary, a competent-looking woman in her fifties, told her when Kate gave her name. 'Come with me.'

Turning, she led Kate down a short hall and rapped briskly on the door at the end. 'Ms McKee is here,' she announced, opening it and stepping aside so Kate could enter.

The room was more welcoming than Kate had imagined. The furniture was all streamlined modern teak, but the shelves held more than the requisite books and papers. On them Kate also saw beautifully crafted Greek pottery, olive wood carvings and a set of jade chessmen. Hanging from the ceiling in the corner of the room was a mobile of various fantastic fish, glittering and iridescent, moving gently now as the door opened and closed.

Damon Alexakis didn't seem to notice. He was sitting at his desk, scanning an invoice. He didn't look up until he'd finished it and signed it at the bottom. Then his gazed lifted and Kate found herself staring into a pair of dark brown assessing eyes. He didn't smile.

Kate did. It was the first thing she told all her prospective employees. 'Smile. First impressions are important. And our clients want to know they're entrusting their children to happy people.'

She'd always been sure that smiles swayed people's opinions. She was quite sure hers had no effect on Damon Alexakis.

'Mr Alexakis,' she began determinedly, offering her hand, 'it's a pleasure to meet you.'

He didn't rise, didn't take her hand. He stayed right where he was, his only movement the lifting of one dark brow. 'I can't imagine why.'

The slight hint of a Greek accent she'd been expecting, the cold disbelief in his tone she had not. Kate pulled her hand back and frowned. 'Sophia has spoken of you a great deal.'

'Indeed? And did she tell you I won't tolerate adultery.'

Kate straightened up sharply. 'I beg your pardon?'

He gave a harsh laugh and stood up. She took a step backward. He was far taller than she'd expected. Stephanos was only an inch or two taller than she was. Sophia was a tiny woman.

'Nervous, Ms McKee?' he drawled.

'Should I be?'

'Damned right you should. I know you've pulled the wool over Sophia's eyes. She thinks you're God's gift.' His mouth twisted bitterly. 'The more fool she. But I know different.'

'And what exactly is it that you think you know, Mr Alexakis?'

'All about you. And Stephanos.'

'Stephanos? *And me*?'

She didn't have to guess what he thought any longer. It was all too clear. Be calm, she always told her prospective nannies. Be steady and rational.

Kate saw red. 'You think Stephanos and I——? Let me tell you something about your precious brother-in-law, Mr Alexakis! Stephanos Andropolis is a womanising creep. It's no wonder you can't keep a mother's helper, the way he acts! Every one of my girls had the same complaint.'

It was Damon Alexakis's turn to look astonished. Still his eyes narrowed and he paused before he asked, 'What are you saying, Ms McKee? Are you denying that you and Stephanos——'

'I most certainly am!'

He gave a rude, disbelieving snort. 'You didn't meet him at the Plaza Hotel last Wednesday?'

Oh, hell, Kate thought. She knew her cheeks were reddening. It was the curse of her ivory complexion. 'I was meeting my father,' she said stiffly.

'Your father looks a lot like Stephanos?'

'No, of course not. I had met my father for lunch. It was my day off. He was there with a business associate and——' she didn't want to explain this, didn't want to even think about the foolishness she'd committed last Wednesday '—and as we were leaving, I—I ran into Stephanos.'

'Who just happened to be there, too. A coincidence?' Damon asked in a silky tone.

'I don't know what he was doing there,' Kate said flatly. She had only thanked heaven at the time that he was.

'You must have been very glad to see him,' Damon said. His eyes were watching her intently.

'I was, as a matter of fact,' she said irritably.

'So glad that you tucked your arm in his and kissed him? So glad that you went off with him towards the rooms?'

'I never went to his room! I didn't even know he had a room!'

'Of course you didn't,' Damon said with patent disbelief.

'If you think I'm having an affair with your brother-in-law, you're a fool.'

'You're the one who's the fool, Ms McKee,' Damon said flatly. 'Stephanos won't marry you, if that's what you're hoping for.'

'I don't want to marry Stephanos! I don't even like him! He makes me sick!'

'Protesting a bit much, aren't you?' he asked with deceptive mildness.

Kate sighed. She wanted to tear her hair. Damn Stephanos. Damn her father, whose plans she'd been trying to thwart by pretending to be glad to see Stephanos. And damn Damon Alexakis for putting his own construction on what had been an act of desperation on her part, and certainly not encouragement to Stephanos.

The last thing Kate wanted was an affair.

No, that wasn't quite true. The last thing she wanted was to get married—and that was her father's plan.

She ventured a look at Damon. He was looking at her, his expression harsh and sceptical. She remembered everything she'd ever heard about him—how clever he was, how smart, how, according to her father, a man would have to get up damned early in the morning to put anything over on Damon Alexakis.

She didn't imagine he was going to be satisfied with anything less than the truth.

Did she want to tell him the truth?

No.

Did she have a choice? Not really. Not when a man as powerful as Damon Alexakis thought she was out to ruin his sister's marriage. All it would take would be a few words from a man like him and Kate's fledgling business, which she had worked so hard to develop, would die without a prayer.

Her father, disapproving all the while, had at least vowed not to act against her business venture.

'I won't stop you, Kate,' he'd said when she'd announced her plans to open Kid Kare. 'I won't have to. You'll see how hard it is, and you'll come around. You'll stop yourself.'

His certainty that she would fail had done more to encourage her determination than anything. She'd begun Kid Kare the next week, and had worked now for three years. At last she was getting a reputation for placing competent, well-mannered, responsible people in childcare situations.

She was succeeding in spite of his prediction of failure. Eugene DeMornay didn't acknowledge it, and he certainly hadn't ever given his daughter his blessing. But it was a sure sign of her success, that he was now taking another tack—he was proposing a marriage between her and Jeffrey.

There was no way Kate was marrying Jeffrey. Or anyone else. Not after her marriage to Bryce! If her father wanted a male successor, he'd have to adopt one. Kate's future was all tied up with Kid Kare — provided Damon Alexakis left it standing.

'I can explain,' she said quietly now, composing herself as best she could.

'Oh?' Once more he lifted that mocking brow.

'It will take a little time.'

'If it's an entertaining story, I suppose I can make the time,' he said with a hint of irony. He gestured towards the chair facing the desk, inviting her wordlessly to sit down.

Kate did. He sat down opposite her on the other side of the desk. He looked as tough and intimidating sitting down as he had standing up, as if he could squash her entire future with a phone call.

That thought gave her the courage to begin.

'You have, perhaps, heard of Eugene DeMornay?'

She saw a flicker of surprise in Damon's eyes at the start of her story. 'I've met him,' he acknowledged. 'He's a barracuda.'

'Takes one to know one,' Kate muttered. 'He's also my father.'

This time there was no concealing the surprise in his expression. He scowled and leaned forward to look at her ringless hand. 'McKee an assumed name?'

'I'm a widow. My husband died four years ago in an accident.'

He looked momentarily taken aback. 'I'm sorry.'

'I've recovered now.'

'Obviously.'

'By throwing myself into my work,' Kate said firmly through gritted teeth. It wasn't entirely the truth, but she wasn't detailing her disastrous marriage to Bryce for Damon Alexakis. 'After Bryce died, I needed something to keep me busy. I was an early childhood education major in college. I have a graduate degree in psychology. I decided to start Kid Kare because I believe very strongly that with so many families in which both parents work, it is essential for parents to have loving, caring people to entrust with their children.'

'Like you?' His sarcasm was clear.

'Exactly like me,' Kate said. 'And like Tracy Everson, and Stacy Jerome and the three other girls whom I sent to take care of your nieces. But trust is a two-way street, Mr Alexakis. And your brother-in-law violated it in every case.'

He stared at her. 'You're telling me Stephanos was after all of them?'

'That's exactly what I'm telling you.'

He didn't say a word. A line appeared between his brows as he continued staring at her. Kate stared back, determined not to look away.

Finally he shrugged. 'Go on.'

She blinked, then coloured. 'Go on? With what? You want me to tell you what he did?'

A faint smile touched Damon's mouth. 'If you like. Or you could tell me why you were after him.'

'I was not "after him",' Kate said sharply.

He steepled his fingers and looked at her over the tops of them. 'Then suppose you tell me what you were doing.'

Kate sighed. 'I had just finished having lunch with my father and his associate, Jeffrey Hardesty. We were having a slight. . .difference of opinion, and I. . .well, I. . .needed an excuse to get away. I looked up and saw Stephanos. I don't know why he was there. But I went up to him and I——' she stopped for a moment, gathering courage, then plunged on '—I acted more enthusiastic about seeing him than I felt.'

'Linked arms with him? Kissed him? That sort of thing?' The sarcasm was evident in every word.

'I didn't kiss him. He—he kissed me,' she muttered,

looking down at her fingers for a moment before lifting her gaze and staring at him, defying him to dispute it.

'And if I believe that, you're going to sell me the Acropolis, right?'

'Oh, forget it!' Kate got to her feet. 'I don't know why I'm bothering. You've already decided what sort of person I am. And given that, no doubt you'll convince Sophia to fire me. Well, fine. I'll save you the trouble. I quit.' She turned and started for the door.

'Ms McKee!' His voice cracked through the air like a whip. 'Sit down.'

She barely glanced over her shoulder. 'No, thank you.' She reached for the doorknob.

A second later, she was nudged aside and Damon Alexakis had positioned himself between her and the door.

'I said, sit down.' The words were measured and menacing.

Kate didn't budge. 'I'm not one of your employees, Mr Alexakis. I don't have to obey you.' She met his gaze defiantly.

He was standing so close now that she could count the breaths he took, could see the tautness around his mouth and could even notice the way a muscle ticked in his jaw. She wanted to take a step back. She stood her ground. 'We teach children politeness, Mr Alexakis. Did no one teach you?'

She saw his mouth tighten even further. 'Please, Ms McKee,' he said after a long moment. 'Sit down.'

There was no sarcasm in his tone this time, but no friendliness either. He had given an inch, but no more.

'I won't sit here listening to you throw accusations at me.'

'But I should sit here and listen to you throw them at Stephanos?'

'You accused him first.'

A corner of his mouth twisted when he caught her point. 'So I did.'

'Then do my accusations seem entirely unreasonable?'

He shoved a hand through his black hair. 'I don't know. I suppose not,' he said reluctantly. 'But some of those girls were no more than sixteen!'

'They were at least eighteen, all of them. I only place adults. Not that that excuses your brother-in-law,' Kate added quickly.

'Why do you keep sending them, if he's such a lecher?'

'I'm not sending them for him! Your sister needs someone to help with the girls. And——' Kate gave a tiny shrug '——placing a mother's helper in such a prestigious family would be a coup for the agency. The business is only three years old. We need all the recommendations we can get. Besides, it was a matter of pride.'

'No job too dirty?'

Kate flushed. 'Something like that.'

'So you took it on yourself?'

'I thought perhaps he was attracted because the girls were relatively young.'

'And you're so old.'

'I'm twenty-eight.'

'A veritable ancient,' he mocked.

'Old enough to handle your brother-in-law.'

'Apparently not. He doesn't seem to be able to keep his hands off you, according to Alice.'

Alice was the cook. Kate wondered how many other spies Damon had in his network.

'He will. I'll make sure of it. I hadn't intended to be there long anyway. I have a perfect woman for the job, Mrs Partridge. She's nearly sixty. A delightful grandmotherly type. Unfortunately she's finishing up a temporary assignment at the moment and so I was filling in.'

Damon didn't comment on that. He cocked his head. 'Tell me more about this disagreement with your father.'

Kate groaned inwardly, having hoped he'd forgotten about that. 'It wasn't important.'

'Liar.'

Kate bristled. 'What makes you say that?'

'Either you're having an affair with Stephanos or you're using him as a decoy to get away from Daddy. Which is it?'

'He had just suggested that Jeffrey and I get married,' she admitted.

'What did Jeffrey have to say?'

'He didn't. Not then. But I suppose he was willing.' She was crimson, embarrassed as usual at the crassness of her father's tactics.

'And you weren't?'

'No!'

'Not in love with Jeffrey?'

'Certainly not. Besides, I'm not interested in marrying again. I don't want any husband.'

He considered that. She knew what he was concluding—that she had loved Bryce too much, that she was sure she'd never love again and be able to replace him. It was what everyone thought, and Kate was quite willing to let them think it.

'Interesting,' Damon said. He looked at her assessingly for a moment, then his gaze moved to the chair. 'If I move away from the door are you going to bolt again?'

'Are you through accusing me?'

He nodded. 'For the moment.'

Kate, who had begun to relax, stiffened again at his words.

He smiled grimly. 'Sit down, Kate McKee. We have things to talk about.'

'What things?'

He nodded at the chair and moved towards the desk himself. But this time, instead of sitting down behind it, he hitched one hip up on the corner of it and waited until she'd come and sat.

'Things like what you told your father when you hit on — excuse me — when you "approached" Stephanos so, shall we say, enthusiastically.'

'What difference does that make?'

'It makes a difference.'

'I don't see how,' she said stubbornly.

'Tell me.'

'Oh, good grief. You can guess, can't you?' She glared at him irritably.

'I can make a fair stab at it, yes. Something about not possibly being able to marry Jeffrey because Stephanos was your man?' He said it all with just enough mockery in his voice to make her cringe.

'Something like that,' Kate mumbled, mortified to hear it all spelled out. It had been such a spur-of-the-moment thing! And so incredibly stupid. She had been horrified at her father's suggestion, had made desperate excuses, met her father's doubting gaze, then glanced up and spotted Stephanos — the rest had simply happened!

Kate had never lied in her life. And with good reason, she thought now, if every time she did so, she was going to get caught up in a mess like this one!

'I know it was stupid,' she admitted gruffly.

She expected he'd agree with that, but all he asked was, 'Did you tell your father his name?'

'Of course not! Do you think I'm a complete idiot?

I just said, "There he is now," and jumped up and ran over to him. I certainly didn't introduce them!'

'What will happen when Daddy finds out you lied?'

She shifted uncomfortably in her chair. 'I'll cross that bridge when I come to it.'

'How?'

'I don't know yet,' she said crossly, looking away across the room. Beyond the mobile she could see the Empire State Building, the lights beginning to gleam as the sun set. She focused on them, trying to blot out the man leaning on the desk barely eighteen inches from her.

'Perhaps I can help you out.'

She blinked and looked back at him. 'Why should you?'

He shrugged. 'I'm a businessman, Ms McKee. If I can help you and help myself at the same time, I think that's good business.' He looked almost bored as he spoke.

Kate couldn't imagine any sort of dealings the two of them might conduct that would be mutually beneficial. But then he was the business tycoon, not her.

'What did you have in mind?'

'I want you to marry me.'

CHAPTER TWO

'Very funny.'

Not only was Damon Alexakis powerful, he had a warped sense of humour. Just what I need, Kate thought irritably.

'Who's laughing?'

She looked up at him, startled. He was staring implacably back at her, not a glimmer of laughter in those hard, dark eyes.

'You can't be serious!'

One heavy brow lifted. 'I don't joke about business matters, Ms McKee.'

'Marriage is not a business matter!'

'Sometimes marriage is not a business matter,' he agreed smoothly. 'Sometimes it's a matter of hormones and pregnancy and some ridiculous thing called love. But for thousands of years it's been an economic decision, no more, no less.'

'And that's what you want?'

'That's what I want.'

She shook her head. She felt as if she'd walked through the looking-glass or fallen down a rabbit hole. Certainly she felt as if she'd missed something vital in this conversation. 'It doesn't make sense,' she said finally. 'Why would you want to marry me?'

'I don't want to marry you. I need to marry you.'

'But why?'

He shoved away from the desk, pushed his hands into the pockets of his trousers, and paced around the room, all vestiges of cool detached boredom a thing of the past.

'I do, that's all,' he said after a moment. He didn't look at her, choosing instead to stare out the window into the deepening twilight.

Kate regarded him quizzically, interested in how suddenly agitated he'd become. 'Not fair, Mr Alexakis,' she said after a moment.

He spun on his heel and glared at her. 'What's that supposed to mean?'

She gave him a faint smile. 'I had to tell you my sordid little tale. Let's hear yours.'

He gritted his teeth. 'There's nothing sordid about it.'

'But there is a tale?'

'It's business.'

'And as the person you've approached to take part in this business, however non-sordid as it might be, I have every right to know the particulars.'

He scowled at her. Kate smiled equably back and didn't say a word. He muttered something under his breath, then raked his fingers through his hair, mussing it even more.

'It's my mother,' he blurted out after a moment.

Kate smiled. 'Ah. I see. Your mother and my father.'

'My mother has nothing in common with your father!'

'Maybe not. As you so aptly described him, my father is a barracuda. What's your mother like?'

Damon rubbed the back of his neck, considering. Then his mouth twisted slightly. 'Holding to a sea-world metaphor? A barnacle.'

'Once she attaches herself, she doesn't let go?'

He nodded grimly. 'Ever since my father died, she's focused on me. Consults me about every damned thing from changing the light bulbs to buying and selling stocks.'

'Well, I can see where that might be a bit of a trial,' Kate agreed. 'But I hardly see how getting married will solve it.'

'That's the other part,' he muttered. 'She's determined to see me happy.'

'Married,' Kate translated.

'Right.' He shot her a harried look. 'She's got five daughters left to marry off and that isn't enough. She's determined to find me the perfect wife. She even says it in hallowed tones: 'The Alexakis Bride'. Like the Holy Grail.'

Kate smiled at his tone. 'Well, in the words of one of our former first ladies, "Just Say No".'

'It won't work.'

'It never does,' Kate agreed complacently. 'That's what's wrong with it.'

Damon gave her a narrow look. She gave him an impish grin in return, then sobered, remembering that the proposition he'd made her was no laughing matter.

'Well, I don't see how marrying me will solve your problem. Married is married, however you look at it.'

'No. Married to you is a business arrangement. Married to Marina is——'

'Whoa! Hold on. Who's Marina? This isn't a hypothetical marriage she's trying to arrange, then?'

He grimaced. 'Not any more.'

'She found her? The Alexakis Bride?'

'Apparently.'

'So, who is the lucky lady?'

He glowered at her sarcastic tone. 'Her name is Marina Stavros. She's the daughter of one of my mother's dearest friends.'

'Your version of Jeffrey.'

'If you like,' he said with bad grace.

'You don't, I take it.'

Dark brows drew together. 'Like Marina? Of course

I like Marina. She's young and sweet and beautiful and everything a man could ask for in a wife.'

'Then why don't you marry her?'

'Because, damn it, I don't want a wife! Not now. And when I do, I'll pick her.'

'But if you marry me——'

'You're a business deal. I marry you and you can stay on to help Sophia, as her sister-in-law this time. I guarantee——' he said the word as if it had a hundred-pound weight attached '—that Stephanos won't lay a finger on you. I also guarantee to send plenty of business your way when we're done.'

'We're going to be done?'

'Of course we're going to be done,' he said impatiently. 'You don't think I want to be married to you forever, do you?'

'No, of course not,' Kate said hastily. 'I don't want to be married to you at all,' she pointed out, in case he thought she was enthusiastic about his little plan.

'Not even to save your business?' He gave her a nasty little smile. 'That is what you've been worrying about, isn't it? That I'll do you in?'

Kate's teeth came together with a snap. 'You wouldn't dare.'

'Wouldn't I?'

She had a pretty good idea that he would. And he wouldn't lose any sleep over it either.

'Plus,' he went on, as if their last exchange hadn't even taken place, 'you get proof positive that you were telling the truth to Daddy and can't possibly marry Jeffrey.'

'But I'd still be married to you,' Kate reminded him.

'In name only.'

Her eyes widened. 'Don't you. . .I mean, is there. . . Do you not—um,—*like* women?'

'Damn it! Of course I like women!'

'Oh. I see. You mean you'll be. . .getting it. . .elsewhere.'

'It?' He gave her a sardonic look.

'You know what I mean,' Kate said awkwardly, aware that her colour was deepening again.

'Yes, Ms McKee,' he drawled mockingly. 'I know what you mean.' He sighed and rocked back on his heels. 'And no, I won't be getting "it" anywhere as long as the marriage lasts. I promise you that. I don't condone adultery. I told you that.' He gave her a level look and she remembered what he'd thought about her and Stephanos. 'Well?'

Kate knotted her fingers together, wishing she was dreaming, hoping to wake up. 'This is the most ridiculous thing I've ever heard,' she muttered. 'I can't think of anything crazier.'

'Marrying Jeffrey?' he suggested smoothly.

'I am not going to marry Jeffrey! I have no need of a man to support me. I have a business of my own.'

'For the moment,' he agreed silkily.

Kate's eyes snapped up to meet his. 'Damn you.'

'Damn me all you like,' he said easily. 'But I'm trying to do you a favour. Stop being such an obstructionist, Ms McKee. It's tiresome. Do you want to save your business or not?'

'Of course I do.'

'Do you agree that Sophia needs help?'

'Yes.'

'And do you agree that being able to produce a fiancé on demand will get your father to lay off about Jeffrey?'

'Probably,' she muttered.

'Then where's the problem?'

Kate couldn't answer that. Everything he said made perfect sense in a horrible skewed way.

'But I don't love you,' she protested.

Damon snorted. 'And I sure as hell don't love you. I told you, marriage has nothing to do with love. It's——'

'Business,' Kate filled in for him.

He nodded. 'Ah, you're catching on. Forget love, Ms McKee. You had that once, apparently. So cherish it. I promise I won't usurp his place in your heart. All we'll be doing is acting out the old axiom: you scratch my back and I'll scratch yours.'

She just looked at him. The room was eerily silent.

'For how long?' Kate asked at last.

He gave her a long look, as if he knew she was really considering it at last. 'Not long. A few months.'

'But once you're divorced, won't they——?'

'Marina's family won't accept me if I'm divorced.'

'I see.'

'Will Jeffrey?'

'Accept me? He'd accept me if I was breathing, I think,' Kate said grimly. What mattered to Jeffrey was getting his hooks permanently in DeMornay Enterprises. She was a means to an end, nothing more. And she suspected her father knew it—and didn't care. He liked Jeffrey. That was enough.

'Well, how long, then?' Damon was looking impatient.

'I haven't said I'll even do it.'

'How long?'

'Six months. A year. I don't know.' Kate shifted restlessly. 'Another marriage to someone he didn't approve might make my father think I was hopeless,' she said, voicing the notion as it occurred to her, musing, considering the notion. It was the first comforting thought she'd had in several hours.

Damon looked at her closely. 'He didn't approve of your first marriage?'

'No.' Her eyes met his defiantly.

'All the more reason, then. Sophia will have what she needs. Stephanos's hands will be tied. And you and I will be protected from our respective parents' meddling in our lives.' Damon gave her a confident businessman's smile. 'What have you got to lose?'

'Plenty, I'm sure,' Kate said wryly.

'If it's money you're worried about——'

'Money is not the issue.'

'What then? Not love again?' His tone gave the word a bitter twist.

Kate shrugged helplessly. 'I don't know. I——'

'Look, Ms McKee, you can sit here and dither all night and never be any more certain. The question is, who are you going to let run your life? You or your father?'

'How about you or my father?' Kate suggested.

'I'm not trying to run it. I told you, this is business.' Damon shot back his cuff and took a look at his watch. 'And I have another business deal to make in a phone call to Hawaii in ten minutes. So what's it to be, Ms McKee? What I'm proposing is a one-year marriage. Are you in or not?'

Are you in or not?

Far below in the streets Kate could hear the wail of a siren, the blast of a taxi horn; far above there was the steady thrum of a jet engine. Right in front of her, Damon Alexakis's fingers beat an impatient tattoo on the top of his desk.

Will you marry me or not?

A myriad images collided in her mind: Sophia's exhausted face, the cherubic smiles of Leda and Christina, her five-year-old twins, the smugly smiling face of Jeffrey Hardesty, the tired determination in her father's eyes, the newly stencilled sign in the brownstone's window that said in elegant silver gothic 'KID KARE, INC.'.

Her baby and Sophia's. Those were the images that stayed in her mind. Sophia did need her, there was no doubt about that. And Kate was glad to help out. Perhaps she was even living vicariously. She would never have a child of her own now. KID KARE was her child.

Her business was all she had—she'd been no great success as either a daughter or a wife. If she lost it, she didn't know what she would do.

And Damon could see that she did lose it if he set his mind to it. She hadn't a doubt in the world about that.

Her father wasn't going to take no for an answer any more than Damon's mother would. He was almost seventy. Old enough to retire, he'd been pointing out. If only he had someone in the family he could trust. A reliable, hard-nosed businessman like himself. Someone like Jeffrey, for instance.

Or someone like Damon Alexakis.

The thought brought a smile to Kate's face. Wouldn't Jeffrey's smug smile vanish if he were faced with Damon Alexakis across a boardroom table?

And what would her father think of Damon? He was certainly more of a force to be reckoned with than the smug, bland Jeffrey. In that way at least he was a man cast in Eugene DeMornay's stainless steel mould.

Even when the marriage ended in divorce, her father's opinion of her could hardly be worse than it was already. Besides, he might not even live to see that happen. He had a bad heart. He was always telling her that, too, in an effort to prod her into suitable matrimony.

'You're amused?' Damon's voice cut into her reverie.

'Yes, I am.'

He pushed away from the desk, standing up and

frowning down at her. 'I take it then that you're declining?'

Kate thought about her father, about Jeffrey, about Sophia and Stephanos, about babies, both human and business. She sat up straight and looked at him with guileless blue eyes. 'On the contrary, Mr Alexakis. I'm saying yes.'

He couldn't believe he'd done it. He sat in the stillness of his office and listened to her footsteps recede down the hallway and thought he needed his head examined.

Had he really just proposed marriage to a woman he didn't know? A woman he'd wanted to wipe off the face of the earth less than an hour ago?

Yes, he thought, and his mouth twisted into a grin as he thought it. He had indeed. And it was perhaps a further sign of his mental befuddlement that it didn't seem far-fetched.

What was a wife, anyway, but one more encumbrance, why not have one who was pert and willowy and had big blue eyes that snapped when she was angry? Besides, Kate McKee was at least destined to be useful, helping out with the twins.

He rubbed his hands together, pleased with himself. It was a great solution. It would spike his mother's guns, take care of Sophia's problem, infuriate Stephanos, and incidentally help out the determined Ms McKee.

Best of all, in a year, she would be gone.

What more could he ask?

'Damon!' Sophia beamed the moment he appeared in the doorway of the living-room. 'How lovely! What a surprise!'

She moved to get up from the couch, but he waved her back down, crossing the room and kissing her cheek. He glanced around for any sign of Kate and the children, but Sophia was alone. She was round and smiling, and Damon thought, albeit grudgingly, that she looked better than he'd seen her in several months.

'How are you feeling?'

'Tired. The baby is kicking me day and night. The twins were easier than this one. But I'd certainly be worse if it weren't for Kate.' Sophia's gaze went fondly to the hallway which led to the children's room where Damon supposed she was. 'So, what did you think of her when you met her yesterday? Isn't she a dear?'

'A dear,' he echoed, allowing a hint of approval to creep into his voice. He had to give the impression of being intrigued, smitten almost, without seeming besotted. 'And very attractive as well.'

Sophia's eyes widened. 'Kate? Attractive?' She looked at Damon closely. 'I suppose you're right. She's not striking really. Not tall. No cheekbones to speak of. But there is a sort of warm wholesomeness about her.' She gave her brother a shrewd look. 'Not precisely your type, I wouldn't have said.'

Damon tried to look hurt. 'Am I so predictable, then?'

'So far. You've always gone for the showgirl sort — the love 'em and leave 'em ladies.'

He grinned rakishly. 'The ones who aren't really ladies, you mean.'

Sophia laughed. 'Just so.' She yawned and stretched and set her book aside. 'So, what *are* you doing here, Damon, at five o'clock in the afternoon. Surely you didn't come because of a fascination with Kate.'

'Can't a brother visit his sister without having an ulterior motive?'

'Some brothers can. Not you.'

Damon sighed. 'How devastating to be so transparent. I came to take my nieces for a carriage ride in

Central Park. I promised them, if you'll recall, the last time I was here.'

'At Christmastime.'

'I've been busy.'

'You are here to see Kate, aren't you?' She gave him an assessing look.

'She can come, too.'

'You're not to trifle with my mother's helper, Damon,' Sophia warned. 'I need her.'

Tell that to Stephanos, Damon thought grimly. 'Don't worry, Sophie.' He turned and headed towards the hallway. 'I'll have the kids back by supper.'

'And Kate?'

He grinned. 'Only if I have to.'

'It's not my evening off.'

'Sophie says you can have it.'

'I don't want it!'

Damon tossed a pair of lightweight jackets at his nieces. 'Yes, you do. Stop arguing. How's anybody going to believe you're the least bit eager to see me if you won't agree to dinner after we dump the kiddies?'

'I'm not eager,' Kate protested. She'd been having second thoughts ever since she'd agreed to his preposterous scheme. She'd planned all day long to call him up and tell him she'd changed her mind. But Sophia hadn't given her a moment to breathe.

Now here he was, bursting into the den, commandeering her as if he owned her, barking orders at the twins, herding them along to do his bidding. She stopped in the doorway.

'Move,' Damon said. He nudged Kate through the door, then turned back to his nieces. 'Hurry up, you two.'

'Yes, Uncle Damon. We're coming, Uncle Damon,' they said, scrambling into their jackets and tumbling after him. The girls were as awestruck as everyone else in the presence of their uncle. If he'd told them to jump out of the window, Kate thought, they'd have asked which one.

'I don't think——' she began, but Damon cut her off.

'You don't have to think. Just smile at Sophia and tell her you'll see her later. There's a good girl.' His hand was against her back and his fingers were practically pinching her as he steered her through the room.

Sophia watched them curiously, a smile on her face. 'It's so nice of you to keep your promises, Damon,' she said. 'But then, you always do. Eventually.'

'I do my best.'

'Are you sure you wouldn't rather I stayed and helped you, Sophia?' Kate asked a little desperately.

'No, no, dear. That's quite all right. I was telling Damon that the baby has been active this afternoon, but he seems to have settled down at last. I think I'll nap a bit until Stephanos comes home.' She gave Kate a little waggle of her fingers. 'You have a good time.'

'We will.' Damon ushered them all out of the room, shutting the door firmly behind him.

'This is crazy,' Kate hissed at him as the girls bounded ahead and pressed the button for the lift.

'Necessary,' Damon corrected.

It was a beautiful afternoon for a carriage ride, Kate had to admit that when Damon ushered them out of the taxi near the carriages across from the Plaza Hotel.

The nippy April winds that had plagued the city earlier in the month were absent this afternoon, leaving almost balmy breezes in their stead. Kate could see beds of red and yellow tulips beginning to open and tender shoots of other young plants peeking out of the warming soil. The buds on the trees in Central Park had begun bursting into leaf.

The girls, skipping on either side of Damon, were enchanted with the prospect of their outing, and Damon was smiling and indulgent as he let them take his hands. Kate, seeing no way out, followed them, apprehension giving way to bemusement — for the time being at least.

The apprehension reappeared when they were bundled into the carriage and she found Leda and Christina on one bench facing forward, while she and Damon were wedged together on the opposite one. The feel of his hard body next to hers caused a momentary quickening of her heart. She edged away.

Damon slipped his arm around her and pulled her back. 'Cosy, isn't it?'

Kate shot him a fierce look. 'A little too cosy.'

. He grinned. 'What's the matter, Ms McKee? Don't you like men?' His taunting rephrasing of her question to him was clearly deliberate.

'Sometimes, Mr Alexakis, I wonder if I do,' Kate said frankly.

He looked startled, but before he could respond Leda pointed to the sky and said excitedly, 'Look, Kate! Runaway balloons!'

Sure enough, more than a dozen helium-filled balloons had somehow been let loose and were floating past the treetops, their bright colours vivid against the cloudless sky.

'And look, there's the zoo where we saw the polar bears and penguins, Kate!' Christina added, bouncing up and down on the seat. 'Have you been to the zoo, Uncle Damon? We're going again next week. Do you want to come?'

'I'm sure your uncle is much too busy,' Kate said.

Damon disagreed. 'Sounds like a good idea at that.'

'You shouldn't make promises you won't keep,' Kate chastised him under her breath.

'What makes you think I won't be keeping it?'

'You're a busy man.'

'Ah, yes. But I'm also intending to be an attentive suitor.'

'We need to talk about that,' Kate began.

He closed the space between them and touched his lips to hers. 'Later,' he promised in loverlike tones.

Both girls giggled.

'Damon!' Kate said, outraged. But one glance at his nieces told her that she wasn't going to get anywhere discussing their agreement with them around. But she vowed to let him know as soon as they were alone that she couldn't go through with it.

At least that was her intention until they dropped the twins off and, instead of letting Kate go in with them, he told Sophia he was taking her to dinner. They went to Baudelaire's.

She didn't know if his choice was made by coincidence or design. But the moment they were seated and Kate opened her mouth to tell him the agreement was off, she noticed that directly across the room her father and Jeffrey were entertaining a group of Japanese businessmen.

Her father seemed equally astonished. When he first realised it was Kate he was looking at across the room, he stopped mid-sentence and stared, then recollected his purpose and continued his conversation.

But throughout the evening Eugene DeMornay's narrow gaze strayed in her direction more often than Kate would have liked, and she found herself determinedly smiling at Damon and keeping the conversation going animatedly. She didn't say a word she'd planned to say to him.

There would be time for that later, she promised herself.

Her father made no move to speak to her or even

acknowledge her during the meal. Kate wasn't surprised. Eugene DeMornay always put business first. Even when she and Damon finished and got up to leave, Kate didn't expect he would do more than stare at Damon with his laser-like gaze.

But when they were within ten feet of the table, Eugene DeMornay rose from his chair.

'Katherine.'

Kate felt Damon's fingers tighten briefly on her arm and was grateful for them there.

Her father stepped into her path and reached for her hand. 'What a surprise! I had no idea you'd be here this evening. You should have said.' He leaned towards her and Kate gave him a light peck on the cheek.

'It was a spur-of-the-moment thing,' Kate said nervously.

'Gentlemen,' Eugene turned to his guests, 'I'd like you to meet my daughter, Katherine and——' He looked from Kate to Damon expectantly.

'Damon Alexakis,' Damon introduced himself before Kate could. 'Her fiancé.'

The two Japanese gentlemen offered polite bows.

Jeffrey's jaw dropped.

Kate's father's mouth opened—and shut. His eyes widened, then narrowed. A muscle ticked in his cheek. His gaze went from Damon to Kate where it remained, harsh and accusing.

If she'd seen the slightest bit of wonder, the slightest bit of fatherly concern she would have denied Damon's assertion. She would have said there had been a mistake, they weren't sure yet, Damon was hoping.

But Eugene DeMornay didn't look fatherly. He looked furious. And if there was concern, it was all for his business and Jeffrey.

Kate pulled her hand away and slipped her fingers

through Damon's. 'You know how busy you are, Daddy. I haven't had a chance to bring Damon by to meet you.'

'I can see I've made a mistake by being so inaccessible.' His gaze went once more to Damon. 'Alexakis,' he acknowledged. 'Won't you two join us?'

'We'd be delighted,' Damon said over Kate's incipient protest. He drew over two chairs from the unoccupied table next to theirs, seating Kate next to him so closely that, every time he moved, his suit coat brushed her arm. Instead of moving away, he moved closer, slipping his arm behind her shoulders.

Eugene watched them narrowly. 'Mr Mori and I were going to have a brandy. But perhaps I should order champagne? To toast your engagement?'

'That would be appropriate,' Damon agreed smoothly. He turned and smiled into Kate's eyes, looking every bit the besotted lover.

Eugene's jaw clenched for a split second, then in a tight voice he summoned the waiter. The two Japanese gentlemen spoke to each other quietly in their own language. Jeffrey didn't say a word. Kate was gratified to notice that there was no smile on his face, smug or otherwise.

She didn't know how much her father knew about Damon. No doubt he'd heard of him. The movers and shakers of the world were always well aware of each other, even if they had never formally met.

As she sat there she could almost see their brains clicking round, adding and subtracting, assessing and defining, deciding exactly in which piegeonhole the other belonged.

She should have been feeling far more guilty than she did. But for once, as far as her dealings with her father went, it was nice to have the upper hand.

The champagne arrived and was poured. Eugene

lifted his glass. 'To my daughter, Katherine,' he said, fixing her with a speculative look. 'A woman of surprises.'

'And passion,' Damon said loud enough for Jeffrey to hear.

Kate choked on her champagne. Her face flamed. She began to cough and her eyes began to water.

Jeffrey's eyes bugged. He sat, transfixed. It was Damon who patted Kate's back, offered her water, and then his handkerchief to dab her streaming eyes. The moment she regained her breath, Kate gave him a speaking look.

He gave her a conspiratorial smile in return, then leaned forward and touched his lips to hers. 'Better now?' he asked softly.

Kate opened her mouth, still stunned by both the kiss and the tone of his voice. No sound came out. Gamely she cleared her throat, then tried again.

'S-some.' But she was never going to be able to pull this off. She wasn't the actor Damon was. 'I th-think perhaps we should go.'

'I do, too, love.' Damon got to his feet and smiled apologetically at her father, then turned to Jeffrey. 'See what I mean?' he said in a low tone. 'She can't wait to get me alone.'

Jeffrey's jaw clenched.

Mortified, Kate stepped on Damon's foot. Enough was enough, damn it.

'Goodnight, Daddy. Nice to meet you,' she said to his guests. 'Jeffrey,' she acknowledged briefly, trying to move away as quickly as she could, but Damon's hand held her fast as he made his farewells, beginning with the businessmen, ending with Kate's father.

'Good to have met you at last, Mr DeMornay.'

Eugene didn't look as if he agreed, but he did manage a frosty smile and a nod. 'Alexakis.' There was a pause, then, 'I'll speak to you tomorrow, Katherine.'

'But how long have you known him?'

'Not long.'

'Where did you meet him?'

'I've been working for his sister.'

'Babysitting?' Eugene DeMornay got a surprising amount of disgust and horror in one word.

'Caring for her five-year-old twins, yes.'

Her father snorted. 'I thought you ran the agency, Kate. Don't tell me things are so bad you have to go out and babysit yourself now!'

'I am doing it as a personal favour,' Kate said, which was as close to the truth as she was going to get. 'Sophia hasn't been well.'

'Hmph. And I suppose Damon Alexakis just happened by one day and fell head over heels?' Her father's scathing tone told Kate exactly how likely he thought that idea.

'Something like that.' If she'd felt a bit guilty after they'd left him last night, today facing his hard words and harsh tone, she felt no guilt at all.

'Nonsense. Pure nonsense. I can't believe a daughter of mine would believe such drivel. You can't possibly think he's in love with you, Katherine.'

'And why shouldn't I?'

'Oh, Kate. Grow up. He wants what you've got. DeMornay's,' he elaborated when she didn't respond.

'He has an empire of his own twice the size of yours. He doesn't need DeMornay's, Daddy.' She said it frankly and was glad to be able to say it.

'Of course he doesn't,' Eugene said irritably. 'But that doesn't mean he wouldn't like it. Men like Damon Alexakis don't take what they need, Katherine. They take what they want. I'd heard he was a clever bastard, but by heavens I didn't think he'd stoop this low.'

At his words, Kate felt the anger surging through her veins. 'Why is it so difficult for you to believe that anyone might want me for myself?'

Her father gave a short half-laugh. 'The way Bryce did?'

His words were like a knife slipped between her ribs. Bryce. Oh, yes, Bryce. Her first love. The man she'd adored. The man she'd run away with, had promised to live happily ever after with.

The man who, when he found out her father wasn't going to give them a penny, had left her flat. She supposed she was lucky that only she knew. Her father had always suspected, of course, but it had happened so quickly, he'd never found out. Bryce's fury, fuelled by drink, had led him to drive too fast. Kate became a widow only hours after she'd become an abandoned wife. She'd kept the knowledge to herself.

She spoke to her father now with as indifferent a voice as she could muster. 'Damon and Bryce are different people.'

'Alexakis is a damn sight smarter, I'll grant you that. But he's still not getting his hands on DeMornay's. I pick my successor, Katherine. Not you.'

'I never intended to pick your successor. I only want to pick my own husband. And I've done so.'

'The more fool you,' Eugene rasped, and hung up.

CHAPTER THREE

'DON'T you think you're being excessively attentive?' Kate asked Damon the following afternoon. 'This is the second day in a row you've spirited me away, for goodness' sake. What's Sophia going to think?'

'Exactly what I want her to think — that I'm mad about you.'

Kate gave a muffled snort. 'Even Sophia isn't that gullible.'

'Sophia's a romantic, my dear. That's why she ended up with a fool like Stephanos.'

Kate shook her head. She was a cynic herself as far as love was concerned. Who wouldn't be after having fallen for Bryce? But Damon Alexakis was worse than she was by far.

She glanced out the window now, frowning as she noticed that the taxi was heading uptown towards the Tri-borough Bridge rather than into the heart of the city. 'Where are we going?'

'Reno.'

'Is that a new restaurant?'

'It's a city. In Nevada.'

Kate's head whipped around and she stared at him. 'Reno, Nevada? You're joking.'

'I'm not.'

'Surely you don't expect us to get married. . .today?' Kate couldn't imagine why else they'd be going to Reno, but she hoped she was wrong. She wasn't.

'I do.' Damon smiled a bit sardonically. 'You see. I already know my line.'

'But—I thought you meant weeks from now! I don't want——'

'Sophia needs you right away. I want things settled so Stephanos knows right where he stands.'

'But——' Kate stopped, her mind spinning as she tried to fathom this sudden push towards matrimony. He hadn't even hinted at it last night when he dropped her off. She looked at him suspiciously. 'What happened?'

He shifted uncomfortably. 'What do you mean? Nothing happened. We already agreed on this. I'm only getting the ball rolling.'

'You didn't mention a word about it yesterday. So what happened in the meantime? Is Marina on her way?'

Damon gritted his teeth.

Kate gave him a knowing smile. 'I thought so.'

'They'll be here in a week.'

'So give me an engagement ring.'

Damon shook his head. 'Won't work. A brief engagement is worse than no engagement at all. My mother will know it's a dodge. An engagement ring won't even slow her down. A wedding-ring will. So we're getting married.'

'It's insane,' Kate muttered.

'It's business,' Damon said flatly. 'And don't you forget it.'

Kate was hardly likely to. Damon wasn't acting like any of the other prospective grooms standing idly outside the fake New England wedding chapel that night.

While the others were holding their fiancée's hand, nibbling their ears, sneaking kisses as they waited their turn, Damon was reading the pre-nuptial agreement his lawyer had sent along, stopping now and then to stick his cellular phone to his ear and check on the wording of certain clauses.

Kate sat at the far end of the bench and twiddled her thumbs. So what if everyone was giving them odd looks? she thought.

This marriage, farce though it was, had more going for it than her last one had.

Finally Damon said, 'It'll do the way it is. Don't worry.' He cut off the connection, punched out another number, and began another conversation, this one about a crystal shipment that hadn't arrived from Venice before he left New York.

Kate sighed and sank lower in her seat.

'Mr Alexakis? Miss McKee?' An elderly lady appeared in the doorway to the chapel and looked expectantly at the waiting couples.

'It's not going to spoil if it sits there overnight. It's glass, not eggs,' Damon said into the phone, not paying the least attention to the summons.

Kate wished she hadn't been either. She wished she could blot the whole thing out, go home, and wake up in the morning to find out it was all a bad dream.

'Alexakis,' the woman said more loudly, consulting her list. 'McKee? Are you still here?'

'Here,' Kate said wearily, getting to her feet and looking at Damon. The woman's gaze followed her own, then she shook her head sadly.

'I told you that yesterday, Spiros,' Damon said impatiently. 'I have to go. Talk to you later.' He rang off, bounded to his feet, tucked the phone into the pocket of his suit coat and grabbed Kate's hand. 'Let's get this over with.'

Kate thought that if there was a prize given to the woman who married most unpromisingly, she would have won both times, hands down.

At her first wedding Bryce had been glancing over

his shoulder at every second, as if he expected her father to come striding into the Justice of the Peace's office with a shotgun and blow him away. At her second Damon stood like a mannequin, unmoving and unblinking, as if only the shell of the man was present, but the real Damon Alexakis wasn't there at all.

Probably, Kate thought grimly, he wasn't.

He was probably deep in mental machinations about some business deal that he was in the middle of. Why else would he pause so long when the minister asked him if he took her for his wife, for pity's sake?

Was he thinking they should have signed that pre-nuptial agreement, limiting her access to the Alexakis millions? Was he thinking about the meaning of the vow he was about to make? Was he considering the implications, even at the last moment, of what it meant to take someone for richer and poorer, in sickness and health, promising to love and honour her all the days of his life?

Was he coming to his senses at last?

Kate shot him a quick look.

The minister persisted in his long one, finally clearing his throat.

'I do,' Damon said suddenly. His voice was clipped, his tone brisk. There was no faltering, no hesitancy. It had all been a product of her overactive imagination, Kate told herself.

The minister turned to her. 'Do you, Katherine, take Damon——?'

She could say no. She had a choice. She could put an end to the foolishness here and now. She could act like the adult she considered herself most of the time.

And she could find herself with a bankrupt company, a chortling father, and a smug Jeffrey Hardesty just waiting for her to say yes.

A choice?

Who did she think she was kidding?

She felt Damon's fingers tighten on hers and was suddenly aware that the minister had stopped speaking, that he and Damon were both looking directly at her.

Kate swallowed. 'I do,' she said.

'I hope you weren't expecting a honeymoon,' Damon said, pouring her a glass of celebratory champagne as the jet left the runway on its return trip to New York.

Kate took the glass when he handed it to her. 'Hardly. I wasn't expecting to get married.'

Damon lifted his glass in toast. 'Life is full of surprises.'

Kate gave him a narrow look. 'I bet you aren't as philosophical when they happen to you.'

'I try to anticipate,' Damon agreed. 'To us.' He clinked his glass against hers. Kate lifted her glass to her lips and sipped in silence. It seemed a farce, a toast to foolishness. She had done it, but she couldn't celebrate it.

'Now what?' she said to Damon.

He glanced at his watch. 'We should be back in the city by dawn. I'll drop you off at Sophia's before I go to the office. I'll call a mover and have your things brought to my place in the afternoon. Then I'll be back to pick you up when I get done at the office.'

Kate stared. 'Wait a minute. What do you mean, call the mover? I never agreed to that! I have my own apartment!'

'And you can move back there. After the divorce. For lord's sake, Kate, you can't believe anyone's going to think this is a real marriage if you stay at Sophia's, and keep your things at your apartment.'

'Who cares what they think as long as you don't have to marry Marina?'

Damon's jaw tightened. 'My mother, for one. I need her to think this is a real marriage. She'll raise holy hell if she thinks I've done it to thwart her.'

'And you're afraid of your mother?'

'I'm not afraid of anyone. I respect her, though. And I don't want to hurt her?'

'You don't think marrying someone other than her choice is going to hurt her?'

He rubbed a hand through his hair. 'Maybe it will. Hell, I don't know. But there's a line a man has to draw between letting people run his life and making them happy.'

'And you, of course, never run anyone else's life.'

He ignored her sarcasm. 'I didn't ask you to marry me in order to hurt you.' The look on his face was earnest and intent, surprising Kate in its sincerity.

'I know,' she muttered. 'It's just—I'm just—not used to it yet, I guess.' She gave him a weak smile and a little shrug. 'Sorry. I'm not as good at these machinations as you are.'

He grimaced. 'It's too bad we had to stoop to them. If it wasn't for your father and my mother——'

'And Stephanos. And Jeffrey. And Marina.'

Damon's mouth twisted. 'Right. Well, it won't last forever. A year and it will be a bad memory.'

'How comforting.'

'I wasn't trying to be comforting,' Damon said flatly. 'I was being realistic.'

'So you were.' Kate leaned back in the seat and shut her eyes, suddenly weary. The adrenalin that had kept her going strong throughout the earlier flight, their thirty-minute taxi ride, twenty-minute wedding and subsequent return to the plane slipped away.

She didn't want to trade remarks with Damon Alexakis any longer. She didn't want to even think about the man who was—heaven help her—her husband. He seemed to feel the same way.

'I'll let you rest,' he told her, getting to his feet. 'I've got some contracts to read over.'

Kate didn't think she'd sleep. But she must have, for the first thing she noticed upon opening her eyes was that the city lay sprawled below them, a blanket of twinkling lights, and far out to the east the first rays of sun were beginning to turn the sky a faint pink.

She shifted and stretched, turned her head and noticed that Damon had returned and was sitting next to her again.

He must have brought back the papers he intended to work on, but they lay untouched in his lap and he, too, had fallen asleep. His face was turned towards hers, his eyes shut, his lips slightly parted.

Kate allowed herself the luxury of studying him closely for the first time. According to the forms they'd filled out, he was thirty-four. Her initial impression was that they'd been hard years. For the first time now she actually found herself thinking he looked younger than his age. His mouth looked gentler, his lips fuller. The silky half-moon lashes that touched his cheeks gave him an innocence totally absent when his cool brown eyes were assessing the world at large. He had shed his suit jacket and loosened the knot of his tie. His collar button was undone, affording her the glimpse of a strong throat. As she watched, his eyelids fluttered and he swallowed.

Kate looked away quickly, not wanting to be caught staring if he opened his eyes. But he only shifted his position as the plane banked. His head now rested against her shoulder. She didn't move away.

'Sell it,' he muttered. His jaw tightened. He scowled in his sleep.

Kate smiled a bit wryly, wondering if he ever got away from Alexakis Enterprises. It didn't look like it.

She certainly didn't know much about this man she'd wed. She wasn't sure she wanted to. He wasn't her type at all. He reminded her altogether too much of her father.

She wondered how much luck they would have convincing his family that he'd fallen madly in love with her and she with him. Perhaps they were more gullible than her father had been.

Damon had done his best with her father, that was certain. It wasn't his fault that Eugene DeMornay hadn't believed for a minute that Damon was serious.

What would the old barracuda, as Damon had called him, say when he found out that she and Damon had actually gone through with it? She stifled a laugh.

'Things looking up, are they?' Damon's voice was husky with sleep. He seemed in no hurry to lift his head as he regarded her through bloodshot eyes.

Startled at the sound of his voice, Kate turned to look at him. The hint of innocence was gone. The mouth was thin again, the jaw hard. But she couldn't quite forget the other, younger man she'd glimpsed when he was asleep.

She shifted so that he had to lift his head. 'Just thinking about what our families are going to say. Sophia, Stephanos. Your mother. Your sisters. My father. Jeffrey.'

Damon's mouth twisted. 'I'm sure it'll be interesting.'

'Married? To Damon?' Sophia stared, then began to giggle. 'Oh, my. Oh, my dear!'

'You're married? to *K-Kate*?' Stephanos's face went white. He licked his lips nervously and eased his collar away from his neck.

'Married? Damon's *married*? To who?' One of the sisters stood stock-still and stared. Electra, Kate thought. She wasn't sure. It didn't matter. The three they'd found had said more or less the same thing.

'Married? Oh, for heaven's sake, Kate.' For once Jeffrey didn't look smug at all.

'You never learn, do you, Katherine? Well, it's your bed. Lie in it.' Eugene DeMornay shook his head. He walked them to the door of his office, holding Kate back for a moment after Damon had gone ahead. 'If Jeffrey's still here when Alexakis divorces you, we can see if he'll have you then.'

Kate didn't reply. She was too tired.

She and Damon had gone straight from the airport to beard them all, one after another, starting with Sophia and Stephanos at breakfast. They'd moved on to whichever of Damon's sisters he could find, then driven straight to the head office of DeMornay Enterprises. Kate hadn't wanted to, protesting that it was already mid-afternoon and surely it could wait. But Damon had insisted.

In retrospect, Kate supposed she was glad they'd gone. Now, except for telling Damon's mother on Friday, the hard part was over with.

Their families' reactions had hardly been surprising. Still Kate found she was trembling by early evening when Damon took her back to her apartment to get an overnight case.

The moment she opened the door she felt her strength desert her. She'd only been home one night a week since she'd started taking care of the twins, but this was the closest thing to a refuge she had, and now she sank down on the sofa in blessed relief.

Damon stood silently right inside the door, staring down at her, his expression brooding. Kate shut her eyes.

'Don't go to sleep,' Damon said. 'Get what you need and let's go.'

'Can't,' Kate mumbled. She wanted nothing more than to crawl into her bed, pull the covers over her head and not surface again until Christmas. Perhaps not even then.

'We've been through that. You're coming with me. If they call looking for us and we're not there——'

'We could pretend we weren't answering the phone.'

'My housekeeper will.'

'So let's both stay here. I know it's not a penthouse, but it's comfortable,' Kate said quickly. 'Besides, don't you think it will be better to let her tell them we're gone? After all, who would be expecting us to spend the first night we're home chaperoned by a house-keeper? Here we have the place all to ourselves. Much more romantic,' she added wryly.

One of Damon's brows lifted. 'And that's what you want?'

'Of course not. I want to sleep in my own bed.' Kate yawned hugely. 'I'm sorry.' She gave him a wan smile. 'I'm afraid I'm not a very good co-conspirator.'

Damon hesitated, pacing around the small living-room, rubbing a hand through his hair. Finally he sighed. 'Maybe you're right. OK. One night.'

Kate smiled, this time with more enthusiasm. She hauled herself to her feet. 'I'll make up the sofa for you. It won't take a minute.'

Damon stared at her. 'The sofa?'

She stopped and stared at him. 'This is a one-bedroom apartment.'

'I'm supposed to spend my wedding-night on a sofa?'

'You spent your wedding-night on a jet,' she reminded him with some asperity. 'You're the one who wanted to get back as quickly as possible. Besides, this marriage is business, remember?'

Heaven help her, he couldn't be thinking of changing the rules now, could he?

'Right,' Damon muttered. He dropped down on the sofa and grimaced, then began to take off his shoes.

Kate went into the bedroom and sank down on to the bed. She felt as if she'd been awake forever. She kicked off her shoes, then stood up again to shed the wrinkled shirtwaister she'd been wearing for the last thirty-six hours.

Going into the bathroom, she splashed water on her face, ran a brush through her hair, then slipped on a thin cotton nightgown and a pale blue terrycloth robe. Feeling almost human once more, she grabbed clean sheets and a pillow and went back to the living-room.

Damon was lying on the sofa, his tie loose, his collar button open. His eyes had been closed, but when he heard her approach he opened them. The clear male admiration in his gaze made Kate suddenly self-conscious.

'I was grubby. I needed a change.'

'Am I complaining?'

She ignored the appreciation in his voice. Damon Alexakis wasn't interested in her—not that way. Not really. He already had her in the only way that mattered to him: on a marriage licence. She wasn't his type. When it came time to choose the real Alexakis Bride, she was sure the woman would be nothing like her.

'Get up, and I'll make the bed for you.'

He stood, scowling now, his gaze never leaving her. Kate had seen pictures of him in the business weeklies where he looked like that—a sort of dangerous modern-day pirate. Not a man to tangle with.

She turned her back, trying to pretend he was just another overnight guest, like her college roommate Missy or her prep school friend, Antonia. But when he cleared his throat, it was difficult to pretend he was anything less than he was—a strong, virile adult male.

She tried to forget he was also her husband.

No matter what he'd said about how businesslike their arrangement was, she couldn't help but recall how married couples often spent the night.

'Are you hungry? You can check the fridge if you want, but I doubt if there's much here. I've been eating most of my meals at Sophia's.' She knew she was babbling. She couldn't help it.

'I'm not hungry.' His voice was flat.

Kate ventured a sideways glance in his direction. He was staring at the cleavage where her robe gapped. 'Are you th-thirsty?'

'I'm fine.' His voice was brusque. He stepped around her, careful not to touch her, snatched up one of the pillows and shoved it into the pillowcase. 'Let's get on with this.'

They made up the bed together, not speaking. When they finished, Kate nodded towards the bathroom. 'There are fresh towels in the cupboard and new toothbrushes in the medicine cabinet.'

'You have a lot of sleep-over guests, do you?'

'Sometimes I have friends who——'

'Spare me the details,' he said harshly. 'Just remember: there won't be any "sleep-over" guests while you're married to me.'

Kate stared at him, astonished. How dared he misunderstand her? How dared he assume——?

Damon apparently took her stunned silence for guilt. 'I told you: there won't be any women in my life while I'm married to you. I expect the same courtesy in return.' He fixed her with a hard glare. 'In fact, I demand it.'

Kate slapped her hands on her hips. 'Demand what

you damned well please. I don't have to run my life to suit you, Damon Alexakis!'

'Yes, my dear Mrs Alexakis, you do.' He reached for her then, taking her chin between his thumb and forefinger, holding her so that she would be looking straight into his eyes unless she panicked and looked away.

She wouldn't give him the satisfaction.

'As long as you're my wife, the only bed you'll be sharing is mine. Got that?' he asked softly.

Kate jerked her chin out of his grasp. 'I'm not sharing a bed with you. And you can stop jumping to conclusions. I don't sleep around.' Her tone was sullen. But she wasn't going to let him think he'd cowed her into behaving according to his dictates.

He looked at her long and hard. It was a hungry look, a possessive look. It looked like more than business. 'Good. Then we should get along fine.' He brushed past her and headed for the bathroom.

Get along fine? Sure. Right.

Damon was up and gone by the time Kate had awakened the following morning. The sheets and blankets were folded and sitting on the end table when she came into the living-room. On top of them was a note.

I'll pick you up at Sophia's for dinner at seven. Have your bags packed. Damon.

Simple and to the point.

It made Kate grit her teeth, but in a way she was glad. It meant that things were only business after all. She didn't need to worry. She'd been overwrought last night, thinking Damon wanted her. She crossed two days off on her calendar. Only three hundred and sixty-three more.

She took her bags with her to Sophia's where she spent the day deflecting all manner of questions from Sophia, the girls and, even Stephanos, who was clearly worried about how much she might have told his brother-in-law about his pursuit of her.

By seven that evening she was so tired of trying to play the besotted bride and reply to the countless questions that she was almost ready to fling herself into Damon's arms in her eagerness to get out of there.

Damon went one better. He opened the door, spotted her across the room and, ignoring his sister and brother-in-law completely, he strode right over, hauled her straight into his arms and kissed her.

Whatever Kate had been expecting, it wasn't that.

Business, her mind screamed. It's only business.

But her body didn't believe it for a minute! It reacted at once, moulding itself to Damon's, pressing against him, seeking warmth and comfort and the satisfaction of pent-up desires. It was insane, but Kate felt powerless to stop it.

And Damon appeared to want those desires satisfied as well. His lips were hot and hungry. His tongue slipped into her mouth, probing, tasting, inciting urges that made Kate's mind reel and her knees sag.

There was a masculine clearing of throat behind them. 'Don't start anything you can't finish in the presence of five-year-olds,' Stephanos said gruffly.

Kate froze. Damon loosened his grip, stepped back and held her out at arm's length, a bemused smile on his face. 'I think I'd better take you home,' he said to her with a wink. 'My bride missed me,' he said to Stephanos.

Stephanos glared.

Kate's face flamed. She couldn't look at Stephanos or Sophia. She wanted to sink through the floor as Damon towed her out and shut the door behind them.

'Good job,' he said. 'Sophia was impressed.'

'The hell with Sophia,' Kate muttered, wobbling towards the elevator. 'What'd you kiss me like that for?'

'Why did you throw yourself into my arms?'

'I'd spent the day fielding a million stupid questions about our relationship. I was eager for rescue.'

'And that's how you ask for rescue? I'll be looking forward to seeing you when you're really glad to see me.' He winked at her and ushered her into the lift.

'Shut up, Damon.'

He laughed. 'Do you want to go out to dinner or go home?'

'What I want,' Kate said snappishly, 'is to go to my apartment.'

'We'll go to mine.'

His housekeeper, Mrs Vincent, was a motherly sort, at odds with the chrome and polished teak surroundings that pervaded Damon's penthouse flat. She was clearly delighted that Damon had tied the knot, and was all too willing to turn all the decisions over to Kate. Kate liked her at once and tried to listen as Mrs Vincent explained how she normally did things. But the tense days and sleepless night were catching up with her and she kept yawning and apologising.

'Kept you up all night, I'll bet,' Mrs Vincent said with a fond smile in Damon's direction. He was already on the telephone and didn't hear, thank heavens.

'Mmm, well,' Kate mumbled, embarrassed.

'I'm so glad he's married,' Mrs Vincent confided. 'He needs a wife. And so much better to have one he picked himself. I don't hold to that arranged marriage business his mother was up to. All that nonsense about her finding "the Alexakis Bride". Like she was buying some plaster saint. I tell you, a man like that needs a real woman. A strong woman.' She gave Kate a conspiratorial smile. 'Good for you.'

Kate swallowed.

'Now you tell me what you want, I'll do it,' Mrs Vincent said.

Kate smiled and yawned again. 'What I really want is to go to bed.'

Mrs Vincent laughed. 'Ah, young love.'

'I didn't mean——' Kate began hastily, her cheeks burning.

But Damon hung up then and came across the room. 'She's a hot-blooded woman, Mrs Vincent. Now you see why I was so eager to get her to the altar.' He grinned and looped an arm over Kate's shoulders. 'Come, my love. I'll show you to our room.'

'Our room?' Kate spluttered as he steered her down the hallway, '*Our* room?'

He led her into a room at the end of the hall. 'What'd you want me to say, that you'd be sleeping on the couch?'

'Don't be an ass, Damon. I'm not sharing a room with you!'

'Think again.' He shut the door to the spacious master bedroom with floor-to-ceiling windows looking out across Central Park.

It was dusk and amid the trees she spied the thousands of fairy lights that surrounded the Tavern on the Green restaurant and, above them, the tall apartment houses that lined Central Park West.

It was far better to concentrate on that than on the king-size bed which, even in the shadows, was the focal point of the room.

Damon was putting her bags down, opening cupboard doors, pointing out the empty rod and hangers, saying, 'You can use these. And then you can go to bed.'

'I'm not sleeping here.'

'Don't argue. We're never going to make it if you dispute everything I say, Kate.'

'Tough.' She glowered at him, feeling like a stubborn child in the face of his stony determination and not caring in the least.

'I'll leave you to get settled in. I have some more calls to make.'

'Damon, I'm not sleeping——'

'Obviously,' he said mildly, and walked out.

He didn't even listen! He treated her like one of his nieces, not his wife!

Kate flung her handbag at the door he'd just shut. It rebounded with a satisfying thunk. 'I'm not a child,' she told the door furiously.

It opened again. Damon poked his head around the corner. He grinned. 'Then don't act like one.'

Once more he was gone.

Kate glowered after him. She was tempted to take off her shoes and throw them as well. But who knew what he might do if she did? She contented herself with flopping down on the bed and pounding her fists against the mattress instead.

Why on earth had she let herself get into this mess?

She was as tired as she'd claimed. She was also hungry. Her stomach growled even as she lay there. She wished she'd asked for a meal, but she wasn't about to change her mind now. She sat up and drew her knees up to her chest, wrapping her arms around them, thinking about what she should do.

Getting into bed was tempting. Pulling the covers over her head and falling into the blessed oblivion of sleep seemed the better part of valour at the moment. And yet—and yet her lips still remembered the taste of Damon's mouth on hers. Her body still tingled with the imprint of his. And her mind could not quite ignore the possibility that he might come back and slide into the bed beside her.

And then what would happen?

She didn't want to think about it. She'd had enough of men after Bryce. Loving hadn't been at all what she'd expected. She hadn't, she remembered with chagrin, been very good at it. Bryce had been all too willing to point that out.

She could imagine what Damon would say.

Not that she was ever going to give him a chance!

The door opened and Damon came in bearing a tray.

'Don't you believe in knocking?' Kate demanded.

He ignored her, setting the tray in front of her. Kate tried not to look interested at the sight of the thin slices of chicken, fruit and salad on the plate. Her stomach growled, betraying her. 'Thank you,' she said with bad grace.

She dug in, then looked up at Damon still standing there. 'Aren't you having any?'

'I'll eat on the plane.'

'What plane?'

'I just found out I have to fly to Paris tonight. I'll be back on Friday.'

'Paris? Now?'

'I thought you'd be thrilled,' he said drily. 'You get the bed.'

'Well, of course, but you haven't had any more sleep than I have.' And he looked even wearier than she felt.

'I'll live.'

'I'll go home, then,' she said quickly, setting aside the tray and moving to get out of bed. It was too unnerving, staying here, sleeping in Damon's bed.

'The hell you will! We're married, remember.'

'I'll go to Sophia's. I mean, if you're not here, why can't I stay there?'

'Stephanos.'

'He won't ——'

'Damned right he won't. But I'm not letting him even think about it. You come back here, Kate. That's final. I'll be home Friday afternoon, hopefully before my mother arrives. I'll pick you up at Sophia's and we'll go deal with her together.'

He gave her a quick hard kiss and was gone.

Kate stared after him, tasting Damon on her lips and not the food she had hungered for. She lifted her hand and touched them.

Why had he kissed her? No one had been watching.

On Friday, she told herself, there would only be three hundred and fifty-seven days to go.

CHAPTER FOUR

It was Friday. It was in the middle of Sophia's living-room. It was the moment of truth.

There was only one thing Damon hadn't got right: they hadn't had to go anywhere to see his mother. She had arrived at Sophia's, with Marina in tow, only moments before Kate was expecting him.

Now she stood quaking in the family-room, knotting her fingers together, not knowing what to do or say.

'You mean he hasn't *told* her you're married?' Sophia demanded, when Kate insisted on staying there by herself instead of coming in with the twins to see their grandmother.

'Not yet. At least I don't think he has. He's been gone, you know, and. . .and he's had a lot on his mind.'

'More important things than his marriage?' Sophia grumbled. 'I know my brother. He wanted to hit her with a *fait accompli*. That way Marina——' She broke off suddenly and shot Kate a guilty look.

'That's all right. He's mentioned Marina.'

'And that Mama has been expecting him to marry her?'

Kate nodded, unsure whether she should be admitting it, but needing to be as truthful as possible.

'I should have known. To be honest, I'm glad he met you when he did. It's always been such a big thing, this business of finding 'the Alexakis Bride'. It's so much better to marry for love.' She gave Kate a quick hug.

Kate smiled uneasily, feeling guiltier than ever.

'I wish my clever brother had handled things better.

I mean, what's he going to do, walk right past Mama and Marina, grab your hand and say, "This is my wife"?'

Kate didn't know what he was going to do. She couldn't imagine how he was going to explain her to Mrs Alexakis. She was waiting with trepidation when suddenly she heard the front doorbell and Sophia went to answer it.

'Ah, Damon,' she heard Sophia say. 'Here you are at last. Mama and Marina have been waiting.'

'Where's Kate?'

A second later he was beside her, grasping her hand, pulling her into the living-room.

'Mama,' he said to the woman sitting on the sofa, 'I'd like you to meet Kate.'

Kate had tried to imagine what Damon's mother looked like, dreaming up varying combinations of all the formidable women she'd ever met. The reality was something less. Helena Alexakis was not really very large at all. She wore her greying black hair in a matronly style. Her dress was more comfortable-looking than of the latest style. Kate found herself thinking that her mother-in-law looked as if she might be friendly.

Or would have been until she heard the next words out of Damon's mouth.

'She has done me the honour of becoming my bride.'

The world stopped.

Damon's mother's smile froze on her face. She looked in the first instant as if she hadn't grasped the word. And Kate wondered if she even spoke English. It didn't matter for the next moment Damon repeated it once more, this time in Greek.

'Your *bride*?' Helena Alexakis said at last. She looked at her son, then at Kate.

Kate swallowed carefully, standing very still, not

even breathing, as if any move would cause the room to explode.

'Your bride,' Helena Alexakis said again, and this time she sounded less shocked than bemused. A tiny quizzical smile played about the corners of her mouth.

She considered Kate slowly and carefully and Kate felt as if the yardstick measuring 'the Alexakis Bride' had been taken out and laid alongside her.

Kate didn't doubt she'd come up short.

She tried to remain calm. It was, after all, nothing she hadn't expected. She'd known. She'd been warned. But as the seconds stretched into minutes, Kate thought again that she'd made a very big mistake.

Helena Alexakis looked like a kind woman, a loving, caring woman. The sort of woman Kate had always wanted for a mother. Not the sort of woman she'd want to dupe.

And then there was the little matter of the gorgeous young woman still seated on the couch beside her mother-in-law. The young woman who apparently fit Helena Alexakis's requirements for 'the Alexakis Bride'.

Marina still looked shocked by Damon's revelation even if his mother no longer did. Her gaze moved from Kate to Damon and back again. Her eyes were wide and bewildered. Kate didn't blame her a bit.

Helena's gaze shifted to Damon and Kate felt minutely relieved, even though an instant later he slipped an arm around her shoulders and drew her closer.

At last after another minute of silence and one more consideration of Kate, Helena looked at her son and said, 'So why are you here?'

Damon frowned. 'Why am I here?'

'You just got married, yes? So why are you in New York dancing attendance on your mother? You should be on your honeymoon.'

Kate gaped. She felt Damon stiffen next to her.

'Don't be silly, Mama. We don't need a honeymoon.'

'Everyone needs a honeymoon, Damon. To be together, to bond your relationship, it is important. Especially important since you must not have known each other long?' One thin brow lifted as she gave them a speculative, knowing look.

Damon ground his teeth. 'Long enough.'

'He did rather — um — sweep me off my feet,' Kate put in lightly.

Her mother-in-law smiled for the first time. She got up off the sofa and put her hand out to Kate, drawing her close, away from Damon, looking at her again, smiling more broadly. 'A sweeper, is he? My Damon? And I always thought he was so calculating. Good.' Once more she looked at Damon. 'You need a honeymoon.'

'Mama, I have a business.'

'You have a bride, Damon.'

'Yes, but — '

'A bride of your own choosing, yes? One that you love, obviously. So show her.'

'Mama, I — '

'You have Stephanos. You have Arete. Alexakis Enterprises isn't one man, Damon. You have hundreds of people to make business while you are gone. What do I always tell you? You are too busy. You work too hard.' Helena shook her head. Her ample bosom shook slightly as well. She gave her son a look of fond exasperation. 'You just got married. Go away.'

'No.'

'Yes.'

They stared at each other, stalemated.

'Even if I could get away, which I can't,' Damon

said at last, 'Kate is helping out here. She's Sophia's nanny.'

Helena's eyes got wide. 'Her nanny?'

Damon's chin jutted. 'Something wrong with that?'

'As long as you love her, Damon, nothing is wrong with it.'

Damon swallowed. Kate expected him to deny it. She was surprised when he said roughly, 'Of course I love her, but I can't take her on a honeymoon. She takes care of the girls!'

'I will.'

'*You*? Mama, you never ——'

Helena Alexakis stiffened. 'Damon! Do not argue with your mother.' She paused. 'Have you been married before?'

He shifted uneasily, then slid a finger inside his shirt collar. 'No, of course not,' he muttered.

'Of course not,' she mimicked. 'So you don't argue with experience. In business you listen to the experts, don't you?'

'Yes, but ——'

'I am the expert. I know how important it is to have time together. Your father and I ——'

'Kate and I are nothing like you and Papa.'

'You work too hard, same as your papa. You swept Kate off her feet same as your papa. You need what your papa and I needed—to be together. Alone. We spent a month on Sifnos. That is too far, of course. Let's see. Where can you two go. . .?'

'We'll take a weekend in the Hamptons if it'll make you happy.'

'A weekend!' His mother wrinkled her nose. 'Nonsense. A marriage takes nourishment, care, tending, Damon. You can't begin to start a marriage in a weekend. Even when you are in love it takes time. Besides,' she added knowledgeably, 'if you only go so far as the Hamptons, you'll be on the phone all the time. I know! Buccaneer's Cay.'

'No, Mama.' Damon said almost as fast as Sophia said,

'What a good idea. You can go down early and make sure everything is ready for Thanksgiving.'

'I have things to do here. Important things.'

'More important than your marriage?' His mother looked at him, scandalised.

'Damn it——'

'Don't swear, Damon. It's a perfect solution. We will all be down for the holiday. In the meantime, you will have a chance to spend time alone together.'

'We don't need time alone together!'

'What Damon means,' Kate said hastily, 'is that we don't want to shut you out. We want you to share our happiness.'

Helena squeezed her hand. 'And so we will, my dear. We always go to Buccaneer's Cay in late November if there isn't time to go home to Greece. Hasn't Damon told you?'

Kate shook her head.

Helena frowned at her son. 'It's a small island in the Bahamas. We have a small family compound there that Aristotle bought years ago. My husband loved island living, said it gave him the proper focus.' Helena smiled a nostalgic smile. 'Please, do say you'll go.' She gave Kate a look of such entreaty that Kate could think of nothing to say at all. She looked at Damon helplessly. She could see a muscle ticking in his temple, could imagine the wheels turning in his brain, looking for an escape route.

Apparently he didn't find one, for a moment later she felt him let out his breath slowly and carefully. 'All right.'

Helena beamed. 'Don't worry, dear. Stephanos and Arete can take care of things here.'

Damon's expression grew even grimmer. He gave his brother-in-law a stony glare which had Stephanos taking a step backwards. 'Stephanos had better,' he said icily. 'Arete isn't working for us any more.'

'*What*?'

'She's gone over to Strahan Brothers.'

'Strahans? Why? What did you do to her? Damon, if you hurt her feelings——' Obviously all thought of Damon's honeymoon was gone. Arete was the one who mattered now.

Damon's teeth snapped together. 'You'll have to talk to her about that, Mama.' Kate felt herself being towed towards the door. 'Come on, Kate. If we're going on honeymoon——' he came down with lead feet on the word '—I've got work to do.'

They were almost out of the room, when he turned back and looked at the girl still standing behind his mother. 'Nice to see you again, Marina. What brings you here?'

'I can't believe you did that!'

Damon couldn't either, but he didn't need some elfin termagant flinging herself around his living-room berating him for his manners. He already knew they were appalling. He put it down to stress. Normally he was the most tactful of men.

'You're lucky she didn't kill you,' Kate raged on, casting longing glances at anything she might throw at him. Damon was glad he didn't have knick-knacks. She had to settle for glowering instead.

'Should I have ignored her?'

'In the circumstances, you probably should have. Good heavens, Damon, the girl was mortified! Have you no compassion? She came all the way from Greece to marry you!'

'I'm already married.'

'That doesn't signify. You should apologise! You should have been a little more sensitive to her feelings!'

'I was trying to be sensitive to yours.'

Kate snorted. 'If you'd ever thought I had any feelings you wouldn't have asked me to marry you.'

He grinned. 'You're probably right.'

'Stop smiling. This isn't funny. I don't know why I agreed to this! It's a disaster! And now a honeymoon, for heaven's sake!' She grabbed a pillow and flung it at him.

Damon caught the pillow. *She* thought it was a disaster, too? He felt curiously nettled hearing it. 'What are you complaining about? My mother's taking care of the girls.'

'I don't simply take care of the girls. I run the agency. Or have you forgotten?'

He had, as a matter of fact. He'd watched Kate taking care of Sophia's girls and had thought what a good mother she'd make. He hadn't been thinking about her as a career woman. 'What do you expect me to do about it?'

'You could have said no.'

'You heard her. Honeymoons are sacrosanct. If we declined, she'd know the marriage wasn't real.'

'We have the certificate.'

'But we could still get an annulment. We haven't consummated it,' he reminded her. His gaze shifted to the bedroom door. 'Unless, perhaps, you want——' He gave her a suggestive leer.

Kate grabbed another pillow and flung it.

He fielded it, too. 'Then I guess we go to the Bahamas and make them think it's real.'

Kate muttered something distinctly unladylike.

Damon grinned, unsure exactly why he was enjoying this. It wasn't as if he wanted to go on a honeymoon with her, for heaven's sake.

Was it?

The thought gave his stomach a curious queasy lurch.

'When?' she asked sullenly after a moment.

He tried to shake off the feeling. 'Huh? Oh, the sooner the better. If my mother thinks Stephanos can handle the business, she's out of her mind. But if I can spend tonight and tomorrow wrapping up what I absolutely can't trust to anyone else, we can go Sunday and be back the following weekend.'

'What about the Thanksgiving business your mother mentioned?'

'We don't have to stay for that.'

'But your mother said——'

'She can only push so far. I'm damned if I'm going to stay around for family bonding time.'

'Family bonding time?' Kate looked puzzled.

He grimaced. 'My father started it when he came to America, dragging everyone out to the island to spend time together. He was busy always. Never home. So once a year he would insist. And the American Thanksgiving was a natural.'

'It sounds nice,' Kate said almost wistfully.

He stared at her. 'Nice?'

'I only meant——' she gave a helpless shrug '—that it's nice when a family want to be together.'

Damon looked at her more closely. Was that yearning he saw on her face? He couldn't imagine it. If she wanted a family, she ought to get married and have one. She never should have married a guy like him. 'Stay if you want,' he said gruffly.

'No.' Kate shook her head quickly. 'That would be

ridiculous. Why should I bond with your family when I'll be out of it in three hundred and fifty-seven days?' She gave Damon a brisk nod, turned and headed towards the bedroom. 'Goodnight.'

She'd sounded—she hoped—considerably more sanguine than she felt. A week in the Bahamas with Damon? Kate wasn't sure it bore thinking about, but as she undressed for bed she couldn't seem to stop.

It's not as if it's a real honeymoon, she reminded herself, as she tugged her shirt over her head. She probably wouldn't even see him. Once they got there, naturally they could go their separate ways. And would.

But something had been happening to her since she'd married Damon, something she'd never expected. She was remembering all the dreams and fantasies about marriage she'd had before she'd wed Bryce.

In those days she'd been an incurable romantic—a starry-eyed child who'd had dreams of her prince coming to carry her off to his castle, far from her uninterested father and his economic empire. And one of those dreams, she recalled now, had been a honeymoon on a beach.

She reached for her bathrobe. That particular fantasy hadn't even been rooted in the far reaches of darkest adolescence. Right after she'd agreed to marry Bryce, she'd read a magazine article about honeymoons in the Bahamas.

She knew these articles were nothing more than travel come-ons. She knew the happy couples were not newlyweds, but really professional models from New York.

Still, she'd seen the photos of them frolicking on pink sand beaches, standing waist-deep in turquoise water, their arms around each other, smiling, kissing.

She'd smiled at the sight of them strolling through the foamy surf at sunset. And she'd dreamed.

Bryce had taken her to Atlantic City where he'd lost seven hundred dollars at the tables and she'd broken out in hives. So much, Kate thought, for dreams.

The door opened suddenly.

Kate jerked around, clutching the robe against her breasts. 'What do you want?'

Damon looked puzzled. 'To go to sleep?'

'*Here*?' She knew it was a yelp of indignation, but she couldn't help it.

He scowled. 'Hell, yes, here. And don't try to send me out to the sofa, either. We've been through that. Mrs Vincent lives in. She knows what goes on. I'm sleeping here.'

They glared at each other. In the five days he'd been gone, Kate had got used to having the bedroom to herself. There was so little of Damon apparent in its very stark furnishings that she had managed to put him out of her mind.

Big mistake.

She edged towards the bathroom and scooted behind the door. Then she gave an airy wave of the hand that wasn't still clutching the robe. 'Fine,' she said, poking her head around the door to look at him. 'Sleep. You can have the floor.'

'The floor! Like hell!'

'We've been through this before, too, Damon, and you're not sleeping with me. This is a marriage of convenience, nothing else. We never agreed to. . . to. . .' She couldn't seem to say the words.

'Make love?' Damon suggested, smiling.

Kate scowled. 'Have sex.'

'We didn't agree not to, either.'

She stared at him, outraged. 'You said "in name only".'

'That doesn't mean it has to be that way.'

'For me it does.'

He cocked his head. 'Why?'

'Because. . .because we aren't in love!' Were all men so obtuse?

Damon seemed unfazed. 'Well, no, but——'

'I don't have sex with men I don't love. And I don't sleep with them, either. As I said, you can sleep on the floor.'

'It's my room,' he reminded her.

'Yes, but I'm sharing it, and if you don't like it, I won't.'

His eyes narrowed. 'Is that a threat?'

Kate licked her lips, then swallowed. 'It's a statement of fact.'

'This marriage is as important to you as it is to me.'

Kate deliberately refused to think about how he could affect the future of her business. 'I can handle Jeffrey if I have to. Can you handle Mama and Marina?'

Damon muttered something rude under his breath. He raked a hand through his hair. He stalked to the cupboard and took out a quilt and flung it on the floor.

'You're all heart,' he growled.

Probably, Kate thought. Getting into this mess certainly proved she didn't have a brain.

Torture took many forms and Damon felt as if he were discovering new and varied ones every day since he'd been married to Kate.

Lying there listening to Kate's soft humming in the bathroom as she got ready for bed, Damon felt as if he'd found yet another. Nothing about this damnable marriage was working the way it was supposed to!

He was supposed to have spent the hours he was in Paris trying to close a deal, not thinking about Kate.

He was supposed to maintain a disinterested distance, not hurry back to her, ready to propose a cosy candlelight dinner strategy session for dealing with his mother, and be disappointed when his mother was already there. He was supposed to ignore her, not use whatever excuse he could come up with to touch her and taste her lips.

And he certainly was supposed to fall asleep without a thought of her, not lie on the floor of his own bedroom wanting to creep into her bed!

What the hell had he done, proposing this marriage anyway? It was supposed to be a business deal — pure and simple. It was turning out to be anything but!

And his mother, blast her, seemed intent on making it worse.

A honeymoon in the Bahamas! She knew how he loved Buccaneer's Cay. She knew it was the one place in the world where he could kick back and relax, where he quit worrying about the business and enjoyed himself. The one spot where there were no tensions and no pressures. Ever.

And his mother wanted him to take Kate?

He closed his eyes and groaned. With no distractions, with only sun and sand and surf, he would have nothing to keep him from getting to know his new wife, and his mother knew it.

Damon didn't *want* to know his new wife.

He already knew far too much.

He knew that her cheeks turned bright red when he got angry and that she had one tiny off-centre dimple in the left one when she laughed. He knew that she looked as fresh as a daisy with the wind in her hair. He knew she could laugh with the exuberance of a seven-year-old.

He knew she could charm the pout off an unhappy child and bring a smile to the face of another with a

newly skinned knee. He knew she could stop a fight
that had been brewing, could make Sophia nap when
no one else could, could keep his brother-in-law in
line.

He knew that her lips felt soft and full beneath his,
that her curves fitted snugly against the hard lines of
his own frame. He'd learned those curves when he'd
held her against him this evening as they'd stood in
front of his mother.

And now he knew she sang soft snatches of romantic
songs while she got ready for bed.

She was driving him insane. And all the while the
damned woman sounded as if she didn't have a care in
the world!

Probably she didn't, he thought, his fingers tighten-
ing on a fistful of crumpled quilt.

She didn't have a multinational corporation to over-
see. She didn't have a mother and six sisters determined to drive her crazy. She didn't have a
philandering brother-in-law to keep on the straight and
narrow.

Mostly, he thought irritably, she didn't have a
delightful, delectable wife she wasn't allowed to touch!

Thoughts about her upcoming week in the Bahamas
with Damon would have been enough to bedevil Kate
throughout the weekend. Helena Alexakis compli-
cated matters further.

'She's invited me to lunch tomorrow,' Kate told
Damon on Monday afternoon when he picked her up
from Sophia's. 'She and Sophia.'

Damon grimaced. 'So be busy.'

'It's not as simple as that. For one thing, my busy-
ness at midday generally involves the twins, who
happen to be going to a birthday party. But even more
important, I'm not sure I should beg off.'

Damon looked at her, aghast. 'You want to get the third degree?'

'Not particularly. But I'm afraid it will be worse if I avoid her. I mean, right now she sort of seems to like me.'

This last astonishing fact had been borne in on Kate over the weekend. At the family dinner on Saturday night, Helena had been quite genial, asking Kate about her father, about her schooling, about her plans for Kid Kare. And when Sophia had her mother and Damon and his new wife over for brunch on Sunday, Helena had shooed the twins away so she could once again converse with Kate.

This time they had talked about Kate's first marriage, and, rather than resenting Damon's mother's probing, Kate found herself telling Helena more about it than she'd ever told anyone.

At first, of course, Kate had been wary. But Helena was calm and kind and not given to the snap judgements that Kate had always been used to on the parental front. Anyway, it was difficult to keep up one's guard all the time. Particularly in the face of unexpected acceptance.

Damon grunted. 'I'm glad she likes you, at least.'

'Has she said anything negative to you?' Kate wanted to know.

'She hasn't said anything at all to me. She smiles like the cat in that children's story.'

'The Cheshire cat?'

Damon grimaced. 'That's the one.'

Kate didn't know if it was worry about his mother or something else, but Damon had been increasingly stormy and irritable. At first she thought it was a result of his night on the hard wood floor. But he'd slept on the floor of the bedroom for three nights now without comment, declining her suggestion that they add a

futon so it would look like a sofa, but would provide
him with a bed.

'Don't bother,' he'd muttered.

'I only want to help,' Kate had replied, miffed by
his irritable tone.

'Do you?' Damon had asked sarcastically. 'Do you
really?' And without giving her a chance to reply to
that, he'd stalked out.

Kate watched him go and wondered about how
they'd cope for the next three hundred and fifty-four
days.

She was still wondering when she met his mother for
lunch.

Helena had reserved them a table in a small
French restaurant not far from Damon's office. She
was already there, waiting, when Kate arrived,
apologising.

'No, you are not late. I am early. I stopped to see
Damon on my way downtown. I had hoped we'd have
time to talk, but, as always, he is too busy.' She gave
Kate a conspiratorial smile. 'It is a good thing you are
going on this honeymoon. You can straighten out his
priorities.'

The waitress led them to their table in an alcove on
the second floor. It was a cosy, intimate setting — the
sort that seemed to call for secrets shared and hearts
bared. Kate took a mental inventory, making sure all
her defences were in place.

Then, once they had ordered, Helena undermined
them all.

'I can't tell you how happy I am that at last Damon
has found his bride.'

Kate, about to take a sip of her wine, set it down,
grateful she wasn't choking on it.

Helena laughed at the expression on her face. 'You
are surprised?'

'Well,' Kate hedged, 'he — um — wasn't quite sure how you'd feel about — um — me. I mean, since he hadn't told you and simply foisted me on you.'

'I admit I would have liked to have come to your wedding,' Helena said. 'One doesn't get to see one's only son married every day. But. . .as long as he has found the right woman. . .' Her voice trailed off. She smiled benevolently at Kate, who felt as if she should disclaim all right to being any such thing.

'I'm sorry,' she said in a small voice.

'The wedding, it is a small thing. The marriage, that is what is important,' Helena said. 'Don't be sorry, my dear. Everything is wonderful. Damon has found his bride. I tell you, I was about to give up hope. I was afraid I would have to do it for him.'

'I thought — I mean, he thought — I mean ——' Unable to say what it was either of them had thought, Kate took a quick, desperate gulp of her wine.

The waitress brought their meals. Helena dug right into her bowl of bouillabaisse.

'I was getting desperate, I don't need to tell you,' Helena went on. 'For years I have been talking to him about what he should look for in a bride. She must be strong-willed, I tell him. She must have integrity and strength of character, and a certain sense of joy. All these things she will need to deal with you, I tell him. And I never know if he listens.' Helena stabbed a shrimp. 'He grunts. He mumbles. He goes to meetings in the middle of what I say. "I know women, Mama," he tells me. "I got sisters." And I tell him, Damon, sisters aren't the same.'

Kate laid her fork down and simply listened.

'I never thought he took it seriously. Every time I brought it up, he would get this look on his face and he would say, "More advice about the Alexakis Bride?" and I would say, "Damon, it's important, the most important decision of your life." And he would ignore me. So I told him last time I came to New York, you can't do it yourself. I will help.' Helena crunched down the shrimp with considerable relish.

Kate sat mesmerised.

'I will find you a bride, I tell him. And you know what he says? He says to me, "Go ahead. I have a business to run".' Helena shook her head and smiled at Kate. 'And all the while he was listening to me. He married you.'

Kate wanted to sink right through the floor.

'I couldn't have done better myself.'

Kate hesitated, then had to ask, 'What about Marina?'

Helena made a tsking sound and shook her head. 'Marina is a lovely girl. Spirited. Charming. She would have made a passable Alexakis Bride — I think. But she is so young, so untried in the trials of life. I told Damon I would find him a bride, and so I brought Marina with me — ' Helena chuckled ' — more to irritate him than anything else.'

'Then. . .you didn't intend him to marry her?'

Helena sopped up some of the stew with a piece of French bread. 'If he loved her, of course. Mostly I wanted him to sit up and take notice. To think about marriage, about what he wanted in a bride. And all the time I was worrying, he had done much better than think. He had fallen in love!'

Kate closed her eyes and prayed for divine intervention.

'I worried a little when I first met you. Damon is a strong man. A stubborn man.' Helena sighed. 'But now that we have talked, I feel much better. You, too, are strong. You would have to be, to grow up with your father, to resist his will and marry without his permission. You are strong in other ways, too. You are making your own business. I envy you your independence. It will be good for Damon not to be the only businessperson,' she said cheerfully. 'You must keep your hand in after the children.'

'Children?' Kate croaked.

'Surely you want children?' For the first time Helena looked worried.

'Of course I want children! But——'

'I was sure you would. Seeing you with Leda and Christina was enough to tell me you will be a wonderful mother.' Helena beamed. 'I'm sure Damon saw that, too. I must give my son credit. He has done well indeed.' She finished her bread, then cocked her head and looked at Kate. 'Is there something wrong with your meal, dear? You aren't eating.'

CHAPTER FIVE

'WHAT do you mean, we didn't have to get married?'

Kate finished tossing the salad, glad that it was Mrs Vincent's day off and that she wasn't around to hear this conversation, not that they'd have been having it if she had been, of course.

'Just what I said. You jumped the gun. Marina wasn't a prospective Alexakis Bride.' She gave Damon a bright smile which brought her a glower in return.

'How do you know?'

'Your mother said.'

'*You asked her*?'

'Well, sort of. Not precisely,' Kate added quickly when Damon looked as if he might explode. 'She was discussing all the — er — things she hoped you would find in the woman you married. And then she said she was happy you'd found them in me.' She offered this last a bit hesitantly.

Damon didn't say anything. He leaned against the kitchen counter, eyeing her narrowly.

'She — er — didn't think you were paying attention when she talked about what you needed in a bride. And she's glad you did.'

Damon muttered something under his breath. 'And Marina?' he prompted when she didn't add anything else.

Kate set the salad on the table and took the steaks out of the broiler. 'Marina was — um — sort of a — er — prod, as it were.'

'Prod!'

'To stimulate your thinking.'

The muttering became more furious. Kate was glad it was in Greek. She didn't think she wanted to know what he was saying.

'Sit down,' she said. 'We can eat.'

Damon sat, but he didn't eat. He picked up his knife and stabbed his steak. He watched the juices ooze all over the plate. Then he pulled out the knife and stabbed it again.

'So,' Kate said, 'we can get an annulment if you want.'

Damon's head jerked up. His gaze was as sharp as the knife. 'The hell we will!'

Taken aback, Kate scowled. 'But if you don't actually need to be married to me. . .I mean, I won't hold you to it—I mean, on account of Jeffrey and all.'

She'd given it considerable thought on the way home in the taxi this afternoon, and as tempting as it would be to hold him to his part of the bargain, she decided that it was only fair to let him go.

She could handle Jeffrey and her father, especially now that she had another abortive marriage under her belt, and Damon certainly wouldn't damage her business at this point.

'Jeffrey hell! This has nothing to do with Jeffrey.' Damon was looking at her, outraged. 'Do you honestly think we're going to get an annulment now? Do you have any idea what my mother would think if we did?'

'Oh,' Kate said, considering it.

'Yes, oh,' Damon said with scathing mockery.

'Well, it was really pretty idiotic,' Kate retorted, stung.

'Which makes you as big an idiot as I am.'

Kate muttered under her breath. It wasn't exactly polite of him to mention it, but it didn't surprise her. 'So what do you suggest?'

Damon stabbed the steak one more time. 'I suggest we go have our honeymoon in the Bahamas.'

Be flexible, Kate always told her mother's helpers. Roll with the punches.

Good advice in the face of two-year-olds throwing temper tantrums and capricious society mamas. Not bad when one found oneself confronted with a scowling, grouchy Greek husband, either.

Kate had done her best, despite feeling equal parts guilty and foolish, to face the honeymoon prospect with equanimity. Damon had been alternately brusque, silent and sulky.

Considering that his nights on the floor might be causing some of it, Kate offered to go out and get him a fold-up mattress. He practically bit her head off.

'I was only trying to help,' she protested.

'That's not the kind of help I need,' Damon snarled, and stalked out.

The rest of their encounters hadn't been much better. She hoped that once they got away from work and family, things would improve.

'Damon loves Buccaneer's Cay,' Helena had told her at their fateful lunch. 'It will be the best possible place for you to go.'

But now, as the plane dipped low over the turquoise waters just beyond the Atlantic coast of tiny Buccaneer's Cay, Kate wasn't sure about that.

Certainly Damon didn't look pleased. He'd played the cheerful bridegroom that morning at the airport until his mother and sisters had disappeared, then he'd pulled a sheaf of papers out of his carry-on bag and proceeded to ignore Kate for the rest of the time.

Kate had attempted a couple of conversational gambits, but when they both met with monosyllabic replies she gave up. Be that way, then, she thought, you old grouch.

However bad the situation was, she couldn't help feeling an inkling of excitement, a tremor of eagerness to see this new and wondrous land. She fully intended to enjoy herself. What Damon did was his problem.

The plane banked and came across the island, allowing a clear view of the narrow sand beach and the string of houses that dotted the jungle behind it.

'Which house is it?' Kate asked.

Damon glanced up briefly and pointed. 'There.'

She picked out a two storey, tangerine-coloured stucco building with stone fireplaces, tall shuttered windows, and wide verandas, tucked among the trees. There were two or three smaller buildings nearby. Sheds or caretaker's cottages, no doubt.

'It's lovely,' Kate said.

Damon went back to his papers.

They didn't land on Buccaneer's Cay itself. The airstrip was on a larger island nearby. A taxi and the boat would take them at last to the landing at Buccaneer's Cay.

She had learned that from Helena, too. Damon didn't say a word. Not until they finally crossed the bay and the boat docked at the custom's house.

There they found themselves hailed by a burly black man, and Damon put away his papers and broke into a grin. 'Joe!'

It was the first smile Kate had seen on him all week.

'Hey, mon, good to see you. You down early this year.' Joe shook Damon's hand. 'An' with a pretty lady.'

'I'm on my honeymoon.'

Joe's eyes bugged. Then he clapped Damon on the shoulder and pumped his hand. 'You sure are! A mighty pretty lady!' He laughed, then stopped and

gave Kate a friendly, but clearly assessing look. 'The
Alexakis Bride!' he said after a moment. 'Yes, sir.
Your mother done good.'

'My mother had nothing to do with it.'

Joe looked momentarily taken aback as he led them
to the moke. He started to say something, but didn't.
'Ah. Like that, is it?' He winked at Kate. 'You must
be a pretty special lady.'

For the thousandth time Kate wished she weren't
there under false pretences. She gave him a hopeful
smile. 'I try.'

Joe grinned. 'You got him to th'altar. That says it
all. You got it made.'

'We'll see about that,' Damon said, but he was
smiling, too.

And there was still a hint of that smile hovering on
his face as they bounced their way through the jungle
towards the house. Kate found herself wishing that
smile would disappear.

All week long she'd wished he wouldn't be so crabby
and remote. Now she thought it might have been a
blessing. He was gorgeous when he smiled!

At last the moke halted at the end of the road
behind the huge two storey house Damon had pointed
out from the plane. Its tall, narrow windows and broad
white porches reminded Kate of something out of a
nineteenth-century seafaring novel.

She was charmed. Also relieved. In a place this big
she and Damon would have no trouble avoiding each
other.

Before she could say anything, down the path
towards them bustled a tall, robust woman in a yellow
dress.

'Mr Damon! Your mama call last Monday and say
you got married! Let me see this lucky lady!'

Damon said to Kate under his breath, 'Her name is Teresa, and she's as quick as they come.'

'I'll keep it in mind.' Kate pasted on a bright smile as Damon stepped out and dragged her out after him into Teresa's embrace.

It was like being hugged by a pillow, warm and sweet-smelling, and Kate felt an irresistible urge to return it.

'Let me look at you, honey,' Teresa said at last, pulling back and holding Kate out at arm's length, beaming at her. Kate's gaze slid guiltily away.

'She shy?' Teresa demanded of Damon. 'You don' need to be shy, honey. Not with me. Why, you're just as pretty as the missus said you is. She's so pleased! I always knew Mr Damon would find hisself a beauty.' She turned an assessing gaze on Damon. 'Had to find one to match him, didn't he?' she said to Kate with a grin.

Kate was surprised to see Damon's cheekbones lined with red.

'You're blind, Teresa,' he said gruffly, reaching for the suitcases, hauling them out of the back of the moke.

Teresa laughed. 'You want to eat first or unpack.'

Damon looked at Kate.

She shrugged.

'We'll unpack,' Damon decided, heading towards the house.

'You ain't sleepin' here,' Teresa said. 'Your mama said to get the cottage ready.'

Damon stopped dead. 'The cottage?' The colour seemed to drain from his face. 'That belongs to Sophia and Stephanos.'

Teresa's teeth gleamed in a broad smile. 'No. It don't. It belongs to married folk. You got a right to it now.' She grinned even more widely. 'You don' want to be rattlin' round in here with me on your honeymoon, boy. You want some privacy. Leastways, that's what your mama said.' She cocked her head. 'She wrong?'

'Of course not,' Damon said irritably. He turned and strode up a narrow tree-lined path without looking back.

Kate stared after him for a split second, nonplussed. Then seeing him disappear around the corner of the house, she followed.

'What cottage?' she asked his back. 'What's going on? Why can't we stay in the main house?'

'Because Mother is manipulating again.' He didn't stop until they reached a small one-storey white house. One of the tiny buildings she'd seen from the air. It was set closer to the ocean than the main house. With its tangerine-coloured shutters and narrow veranda, it looked as if it had been designed and painted as a counterpoint to the main house.

It was darling. It was charming. It was homey. It wasn't big enough.

Kate, with sinking desperation, said so.

'You think I don't know that!' Damon almost shouted at her.

Wincing, Kate opened the door and went in. The living-room-kitchen was bright and airy, painted white and fitted out with a table and chairs as well as a white wicker settee and matching chairs with gaily flowered cushions. Ten steps took her across the room and through the only other door.

It was a bedroom. Equally bright. Equally airy. Just as tiny.

With one double bed.

Kate looked at him narrowly.

Damon said an extremely rude word. 'The cottage wasn't my idea.'

'The marriage was. Honestly, Damon, this gets worse and worse. Didn't you think at all before you proposed this stupid scheme?'

He rubbed a hand through his hair. 'It seemed like a good idea at the time.'

'Do you always make spur-of-the-moment business decisions.'

'Of course not.'

'Well, then. . .?'

He shrugged and leaned against the wall, closing his eyes. 'Put it down to stress.'

Kate thought he did indeed look stressed. If she'd dared she would have reached out and touched his cheek, perhaps brushed that stray lock of hair back off his forehead. She stuffed her hands into the pockets of her skirt.

She looked around the tiny bedroom with its soft white walls and light wicker furniture, its lazily spinning ceiling fan and its flower-quilted bed. She couldn't help thinking what a really lovely place it would be if she were on a real honeymoon.

Deliberately she went back into the other room. 'At least you can sleep in the living-room here,' she said off-handedly.

Damon said a very rude word.

He let Kate have the bedroom.

She told him he was a gentleman.

He could think of another word for it. 'Idiot' sprang to mind. And the longer he lay on the hard wood floor and listened to her humming in the bedroom, imagining her with her long hair loose and free, her face freshly scrubbed, her nightgown barely covering the curves he knew were a part of her, the more certain he was.

Damn! What was he doing here?

Damon didn't like it when things got out of control, and there was no doubt that, as far as his marriage to Kate went, things had. Not that Teresa didn't believe in their wedded bliss. She did. But that was thanks to Kate, not him.

Kate had done everything she should have with Teresa, laughing and smiling over dinner, answering her questions with the right amount of eagerness, even appearing suitably smitten with Damon when it seemed to be required.

It had been his own behaviour that had caused Teresa to lift her brows in wonder. He'd been reluctant to touch Kate when they sat on the sofa side by side. When Teresa had teasingly asked him some silly question about his love-life, he'd almost bitten her head off. And when they were leaving and Kate had casually put her hand on his arm, he'd jumped.

Why? Because he wanted her.

He'd hoped that ignoring her the past week would put a damper on his desire. He'd hoped that she would do something or say something that would turn him off.

She hadn't yet.

He saw the light in the bedroom flick off and heard the bed creak. He remembered the nights last week when he'd lain on the floor of the bedroom and watched her slip into bed. Here he didn't even have the pleasure — or pain — of doing that.

He cursed and rolled over. Something small and dark scuttled across the moonlit floor.

He muttered a word as unprintable as the one he'd used earlier. It was going to be a long night.

Night? Hah. It was going to be a hell of a long week. He tried not to think about the year of marriage that lay ahead of him.

When he did, he told himself that it was purely a

matter of hormones. He hadn't had a woman in a long time. Most of the time it didn't matter. Now it did simply because of the propinquity.

Everywhere he went, there she was.

And he couldn't have her.

Damn it, why hadn't he found a woman who liked casual sex? It would be so much easier to be married to her if she did!

He shut his eyes; he dreamed of Kate.

He dreamed of stripping off her nightgown and learning the line of those curves, discovering the depths of her. He dreamed of making love to her until she was senseless with desire. And then he dreamed of her hands on him—light hands, delicate hands—tempting, teasing as they tripped up his bare calf. His need woke him, made him moan.

And then in that half-awake and half-dreaming state, he realised he could still feel that light touch.

It wasn't Kate.

He yelped, leaping to his feet. A palmetto bug fell to the floor and scurried out of sight under the cupboard. Damon stood, white-faced and shaking, stunned and muttering. He spoke English now without a second thought. He'd used it every day, all day, since he'd been sixteen. But swearing in Greek was far more satisfying.

He muttered one last curse and shuddered, then raked his fingers through his hair and looked longingly at the closed bedroom door. But it didn't take much imagination to conjure up the furore that would result if he invaded that sacred domain.

Muttering, he dragged the sheet over and folded himself onto the short narrow settee. He tucked the edges of the sheet around him, letting none of it touch the floor, and willed himself to sleep again.

This time he dreamed of plate-sized palmetto bugs,

of tarantulas and scorpions, of blue lizards and snakes. He awoke in a cold sweat so often that, at last, he gave up and hauled himself to his feet. There would be no sleep tonight, that was certain.

And no point in sitting there staring at the door that separated him from his wife.

Tossing the sheet on to the settee, Damon strode to the door, then let himself out into the darkness.

The moon had sunk lower and was now behind the trees. He heard soft scuttling sounds in the under-brush, but in reality they posed no menace. Damon didn't even think about them. He stalked straight ahead down the path towards the beach.

The tide was going out and there was almost no surf. The ocean lay like a still sleeping pool. Damon walked without stopping straight across the damp sand and plunged in.

To wash off the touch of the palmetto bug, to cleanse himself of the dreams of tarantulas and snakes, he told himself.

And he did that.

But even when he'd swum for over an hour, even when his lungs were near to bursting and his body longed for rest, even when he finally hauled himself out of the water and dropped down belly-first on to the sand, he still couldn't sleep.

Because it wasn't the memory of the palmetto bug that was keeping him awake. Or the tarantulas and snakes of his nightmares.

It was Kate.

'Yessir,' Teresa said with awful cheer as she spooned scrambled eggs on to their plates that morning at breakfast, 'you do got the look of a man on a honey-moon. Them bloodshot eyes and deep sockets is a dead giveaway.' She gave Damon a broad wink.

'Had a lot of experience, have you?' he asked sourly into his mug of coffee.

Kate nudged him with her elbow. If she had to be polite, there was no reason he shouldn't be.

He raised his eyes to glare at her. He'd been glaring at her all morning, ever since he'd come in at half-past seven, looking as if he'd been dragged backwards under the reef, and she'd asked, 'Oh, did you go for an early swim?'

He'd grunted and stridden past her, heading for the bathroom without speaking. A shower and a shave hadn't improved his disposition much. Kate supposed it was the floor, but she could scarcely offer to provide him with a futon here.

'An' what you going to do today?' Teresa looked at them curiously. 'Or shouldn't I ask?' Another grin.

'I don't know about Kate,' Damon muttered, 'but I need some sleep.'

'Honeymoons be like that,' Teresa said unsympathetically. Kate blushed. Damon ground his teeth.

'The trouble with her is she's known me since I was eight,' Damon grumbled when Teresa went back to the kitchen. 'Thinks she can say anything.'

'She's only teasing,' Kate pointed out.

Damon grunted and bit down on his toast with considerable ferocity.

Teresa's light gibes continued throughout the meal, and Kate could see Damon gradually losing control. All his admonitions to her about making sure Teresa thought they were deeply in love would come to naught by his own mouth if he weren't careful.

'Come on,' she said as soon as they had finished breakfast. 'I'm taking him home,' she explained to Teresa, 'before the wild beast emerges.'

Teresa chuckled. 'You do that. Have your way with him.'

Damon opened his mouth, but Kate didn't wait to see what he was going to say. She grabbed his hand and began hauling him towards the door. 'Cool it,' she muttered. 'Just cool it. We'll go back to the house and you can take a nap.'

'Nap?' Damon sounded outraged.

'Isn't that what you said you wanted?'

'Yes, but——' He stopped, as if he'd been going to say something more, then thought better of it.

'It's not a bad idea, actually,' Kate said, warming to it. 'We can share the bed.'

He made a pleased sound. 'Ah.'

'I'll take it at night and you can have it during the day.'

'*What*?' He stumbled over a root and crashed into her.

Kate grinned. 'It's the perfect solution. After all, Teresa is sure to think you need plenty of rest during the day if you're going to keep up your amatory exploits all night.'

'And you don't need it, I suppose?' he demanded irritably.

Laughter bubbled up inside her. 'I'm not supposed to have to work so hard, I guess. Teresa probably thinks I just lie back and think of New York City.'

Damon scowled.

'Don't be a spoilsport,' she chided him, moving on ahead again. 'It's a better solution than you've come up with.'

'I could think of an even better one,' Damon muttered at her back.

She stopped again and glanced back. 'What?'

He looked at her, his gaze hot and hungry, and Kate didn't need to ask again. 'Forget it,' she said.

She wished she could. She was doing her best.

In fact, it would suit her to a 'T' if he wanted to

sleep the day away. They wouldn't have to pretend undying love for each other if he was asleep.

Though she was at pains to deny it, being around him all the time was making her increasingly nervous. He attracted her, and he shouldn't.

She clapped a broad-brimmed straw hat on her head, waggled her fingers in his direction and headed out of the door.

'Stay away from the house,' Damon's voice called after her. 'Teresa will expect you to be here with me,' he added when Kate turned and frowned.

'I'll head towards the beach first, then go to town. Can I get there by following the beach?'

'When you get to the sand, go right. It's about a mile to a path that leads inland past one of the inns. You'll be able to tell—the sand's been swept for the tourists. Follow the path to the water tower. You can see the town from there.' He paused then added, 'Behave.'

Kate looked back at him, startled.

'Everyone will know who you are. Don't say anything we'll regret.'

'I've already said enough that I regret, starting with "I do",' Kate told him.

'Me, too.'

Their gazes locked for a moment in silent battle. Then Damon turned and strode into the bedroom without another word.

So he didn't like their marriage any better than she did. She was annoyed that the thought disturbed her. It shouldn't, she told herself. She should be glad and she certainly shouldn't be surprised.

But damn it, it still hurt.

Because of Bryce, she told herself. It was because she was still smarting over her failure with Bryce. It certainly couldn't have anything to do with Damon himself. That would be the height of folly.

Deliberately she put Damon Alexakis out of her mind and forced herself to concentrate on the island she was about to explore. They had arrived rather late yesterday, so she'd only caught a glimpse of the town as they'd passed through, and after dinner last night there'd been little chance to explore. Still Damon had taken her down to the beach briefly and she was enchanted by what she'd seen so far.

It was every bit the tropical paradise she'd often dreamed of. But if she hoped to lose herself in it, forgetting Damon and her marriage to him, she soon realised that she was out of luck.

Damon was right—everyone knew about her.

'Mornin', Miz Damon,' the plump lady at the basket shop greeted her.

'How you doin' today, Mrs Damon?' said the old man feeding the chickens.

'Hot 'nough, ain't it, Miz Damon?' said the teenage boy working on the outboard motor by the dock.

And when she tried ducking inside a tiny establishment called Rebecca's Pineapple Shop to buy a soda and recover from the smiling, knowing eyes, the proprietor, a jovial young mother whose toddlers were playing underfoot, asked, 'How long you and Mr Damon stayin'?'

Kate gave up trying to pretend it was coincidence that everyone knew her name. 'A week.'

'A week? Only a week?' the woman looked dismayed.

'We have work to get back to,' Kate said apologetically, and was surprised to note that she really felt that way. She liked the islanders' friendliness. She would have liked to get to know them better.

Rebecca finished shelving some cans of vegetables.

She made a tsking sound. 'Mr Damon, he work too much. Always takin' care of everybody else. Don't ever take time for himself.' She shook her head. 'Hey, Silas,' she called out to the men playing dominoes on the porch. 'You hear that? Mrs Damon say they only be stayin' a week!'

Two elderly faces, both with grizzled beards, peered in the screen. One of them gave Kate a sly grin before turning his gaze to meet Rebecca's. 'She a pretty lady. I reckon maybe Mr Damon figure he gonna get the job done in a week!'

'Silas!' Rebecca looked scandalised.

Kate looked at first one then the other, confused, until the man called Silas cackled and explained, 'Only son, ain't he? Son of his own. Stands to reason. . .' He winked at her.

Kate felt the heat rise in her cheeks. She looked about hopefully for another exit, knowing even as she did so that there wasn't one.

'Don't mind Silas,' Rebecca told her. 'He be a dirty ol' man with a one-track mind. But he right. You sure pretty. Family don't be comin' for the holiday this year?'

'Family? Oh, you mean Damon's. I think they are, but——'

'Then you be here.' Rebecca smiled and handed Kate her soda. 'Alexakises always are.'

Kate could hardly say she wasn't going to be an Alexakis for long. She thanked the lady, smiled weakly and went out onto the porch.

'You an' Mr Damon wanta go fishin'?' Silas said as she passed. 'You tell 'im Silas'll take you. Be my pleasure. He not workin' now, is he?'

'He's sleeping.'

Silas chuckled. 'Wore out, is he? Can't say I'm surprised. Always was a hard worker, that un.'

Blushing furiously, Kate bounded down the steps and set off up the street in a hurry. Silas's cheerful laughter echoed after her as she went.

She didn't go in any more shops. She didn't even finish her trek along the street that skirted the harbour. Instead she headed back across the island towards the beach. It had been almost deserted when she'd walked to town earlier. She was relieved to find it was the same now.

She took her time walking back, scuffing through the fine coral sand, composing her thoughts — or trying to — doing her best to come up with a plan of behaviour.

You must act, not simply react, she always told her fledgling nannies. Children can sense when you're losing control.

Kate knew she was losing control. And she was afraid that the whole world — especially Rebecca and Silas — knew it.

She felt guilty for trying to deceive them and at the same time knew that, even if she was, she wasn't deceiving herself.

There was more to this incipient panic she was feeling than simple deception and the resultant guilt it entailed. There was the way she was reacting to Damon.

The awareness. The tension. The desire.

All day — no, all week — she had tried to ignore it, hoping it would go away. She had thought herself immune to such reactions after Bryce. Heaven knew she ought to be!

But she wasn't.

It was foolishness what she was feeling for Damon Alexakis. It could only cause trouble. He wasn't interested in her. And even if he was staying married to her when he no longer had to in order to keep

Marina at bay, he wasn't staying married to her because he loved her! It was simply that he'd look like an idiot if he admitted it was all a sham now.

He certainly wouldn't want to get involved with her.

And for that matter, Kate McKee, she told herself firmly, kicking the sand, you don't want to get involved with him!

Alexakis.

What? She stopped dead, the word echoing in her mind.

Alexakis, the tiny voice repeated insistently. You're not Kate McKee any more. You're Kate Alexakis now. Damon Alexakis's wife.

Kate shut her eyes and shook her head. She didn't want to think about that.

Still, within minutes she would be upon him again. She would have to decide how to act.

Sinking down in the sand, she drew her knees up and wrapped her arms around them and tried to come to terms with things. But it was no use. The afternoon was not made for thinking.

In New York she could have done it. In New York she was remarkably clear-headed and sensible. There she could have shut everything else out of her mind—the horns and sirens, the suffocating heat reflecting off the buildings, the diesel fumes and car exhaust—and sorted out her relationship with Damon easily.

Not here. Here the island breeze teased her hair, like a lover's fingers loosening it from the knot she'd fixed at the back of her head. Here the sun kissed her back and she shut her eyes. She leaned back, lifting her face towards the warmth, imagining how it would be if this really were a honeymoon, if she had really come here with a man who loved her.

She remembered Bryce. *Always* she remembered Bryce.

But somehow here the disaster that had been her marriage seemed remote and ineffectual. It had hurt her once; it had nearly destroyed her. But now its power over her seemed oddly lessened.

Here in this island paradise that, until a few days ago, Kate had never known existed, she felt the pain fading. She closed her eyes and saw, not Bryce's fair good looks and handsome sneering face, but another face — this one darker, not quite so classically handsome — and she remembered the touch of Damon's lips, their hint of promise, of magic, of hope.

She felt tired. So very tired.

She had worked so hard for so long. She hadn't really taken a day off since Bryce had walked out on her. There hadn't been time to. She'd fought to develop her business, to make her contacts, to hold off her father. She put in hours and days and months and, now that she thought about it, years.

And never once had she flagged. Not even for a weekend. The only times she'd left the city had been to see to home situations. There'd never been a lazy Sunday in the Hamptons or a weekend antiquing with friends in Bucks County. There'd never been a Christmas ski trip or a jaunt to Vermont in the autumn to see the leaves. There'd always been work to do. So very much work.

And anyway, it had helped keep the memories of Bryce and her foolishness at bay.

It had been so long since she'd relaxed like this. So long since she'd stretched out on the sand and let the earth and the sun warm her body. So very, very long since she'd felt as settled and comfortable. The sound of the surf soothed her, lulled her, made her smile.

Of course she would have to sort out what to do about Damon Alexakis soon. But first — if only for a few minutes — she had to close her eyes.

CHAPTER SIX

'You stay out much longer, I be servin' you for dinner 'stead of the lobster.'

The words startled Kate out of a sound sleep and she jerked up to see Teresa standing beside her on the beach, shaking her head and smiling down at her.

'You be cooked, Mrs Kate,' she said, her tone a mixture of disapproval and dismay.

Wincing as she touched her now rosy forearm, Kate nodded. 'I fell asleep. What time is it?'

'Dinnertime. Mr Damon didn't know where you were. Them sisters of his.' She shook her head, irritated. 'I thought maybe I take a look.'

'What about Damon's sisters?'

'They been callin' all day. One problem an' another. Can't leave the poor man alone even on his honeymoon. I don' blame you for goin' for a walk, listenin' to all that.'

'Er — yes. I didn't realise it was so late. I only meant to close my eyes.' But it had been two hours at least. And she hadn't stirred. She had dreamed, though, she remembered that much. They had been incredible dreams. Sexy dreams. About Damon.

If it were possible to turn a deeper shade of red she would have done so.

She shoved a hand through dishevelled hair and scrambled to her feet. 'Thanks for waking me, Teresa. Do I have time for a shower?'

'Depends,' Teresa said darkly, 'if that Electra ever get off the phone. You don't got to let him spend all his time with them, you know.'

'I know,' Kate said.

'Ah, good. He finished.' Teresa grinned. 'I serve dinner now. You can shower later. Mr Damon be happy to help you clean up later, I bet.'

Kate didn't want to think about that. If Bryce had found her wanting, Damon definitely would, all dreams to the contrary. There was no point in complicating matters further over a few hormonal urges.

Damon wanted it to be business. So did she.

She hurried up the beach following Teresa's broad back, trying to put her hair into some semblance of order as she went.

Damon was standing on the veranda. He looked hassled and harried and no more rested than when Kate had left. She felt an unreasoned burst of sympathy for him.

Damon looked her up and down, taking in her rumpled, sweaty clothes, sunburnt face and tousled hair. 'What happened to you?'

All sympathy fled. 'I fell asleep on the beach.'

'Stupid thing to do.'

'I didn't do it intentionally.' She waited until Teresa had disappeared into the kitchen and added, 'I got tired of playing the devoted newlywed in town. I was trying to give us some space. And you some sleep, if you'll recall.'

'Sleep? There's a laugh. I didn't even get my head near a pillow. I didn't bloody get a chance!'

Teresa reappeared carrying a bowl of succulent lobster stew and with obvious effort Damon modulated his tone as she dished it out.

'My sisters called,' he grumbled.

'They miss you that much?'

'They miss coming to me for help at every turn.' He shoved a hand through already tousled hair. 'Pandora is stuck in Vegas without a dime. Electra's show

closed. Chloe is in Dar es Salaam and needs me to
wire her some money to get home. Arete quit at
Strahans', came back to our place and promptly got
into a fight with Stephanos about who was running
things. They both called me. Twice.' He leaned his
elbows on the table and rested his head in them, then
lifted his bloodshot gaze to meet hers. 'I ought to fire
both of them.'

'So, why don't you?'

He looked momentarily startled, then ignoring her,
went on, 'The last one was Daphne trying to unload a
truckload of chinchillas on me. And you.'

'*What*?'

Damon rubbed a hand across his face. 'Don't ask.'
He slid back in his chair and closed his eyes as Teresa
left again. 'God, I'm tired.'

'You look like hell.'

'Thank you very much.'

'Always glad to be of help.' If she'd really been his
wife in more than name, she'd have been far more
sympathetic. She'd have told him he worked far too
hard and let his family take far too much advantage of
him. But in the circumstances, she had no right to.

In the circumstances, it was easier to be flippant,
and safer, too.

Fixing her eyes firmly on her plate, she dug in. It
was a savoury, succulent blend of lobster, potatoes
and vegetables, and it went a long way towards making
things right with the world as far as Kate was
concerned.

'It's very good, ' she said.

But a minute or more passed before Damon hauled
himself upright and, muttering under his breath, began
to eat as well.

They didn't speak again until their plates were clean
and Teresa came to clear the table.

'Not much of a honeymoon,' she commented sadly.

Damon's head jerked up at that. He glowered at her. 'What's that supposed to mean?'

'You all day talkin' on the phone, Mrs Damon goin' to town by herself.'

'We don't have to live in each other's pockets, Teresa,' Damon said shortly.

But Teresa just clucked her tongue. 'What'm I gonna tell your mother?'

'My mother?' Damon looked so horrified that Kate almost laughed. 'You don't have to tell my mother anything!'

Teresa stepped back. 'You don't got to yell, Mr Damon. I hear you. I be right here. Course I got to tell her. She askin'.'

Kate saw Damon visibly try to control himself. With considerable effort he softened his tone. 'Our honeymoon and our marriage are our business, Teresa. Not my mother's. I will thank you not to say a word.'

Kate watched with interest as the two stares met, Damon's hard and fierce, Teresa's mild and curious.

Finally the older woman shrugged. 'Not one word, Mr Damon?'

'Not one word.'

"f that's what you want.' Teresa turned almost sadly and started towards the kitchen.

Damon grunted his satisfaction.

As much as in this instance Kate agreed with him, she did wish he'd be a little less high-handed with Teresa.

'It was a lovely meal, Teresa. Thank you,' Kate called after her, determined to be polite even if her husband wasn't.

Teresa turned and beamed. 'My pleasure. You have a good night, now. I be seein' you at breakfast. You take extra good care of Mr Grouchy here.' She shot a quick look at Damon, noted his fierce expression, giggled and vanished into the kitchen.

'God, I don't know what's got into that woman,' he complained, shoving his chair back and heading for the door. 'She never used to be so cheeky.'

'She's pleased for us.'

Damon snorted. 'She has a damned funny way of showing it.'

'She thinks we're madly in love and she's enchanted.'

'The more fool she,' Damon muttered and strode towards the cottage without looking back.

Kate hurried to catch up. 'Dibs on the shower.'

He glanced back briefly, his expression distasteful. 'You could use one.'

'How gallant of you to say so.'

He gave her a twisted smile. 'Always glad to be of help.' His echo of her earlier words mocked her as she hurried past.

Damn it, she groused as she undressed, why did it have to be like this? Why did they have to continually snipe at each other? Why couldn't they get along?

Kate couldn't ever remember a man who could provoke her the way Damon could. Nor a man who attracted her quite so much either.

She didn't want to think about that.

Deliberately she turned on the water as hard as it would go, stepped under the shower and welcomed a cleansing rush of water beating down on her naked body.

She didn't know how long she stayed there.

Long enough, she hoped, to get herself firmly under control, long enough to tamp down all interest in Damon Alexakis, long enough to recite the list of every nanny she had ever placed, every family she had ever served, every goal she had set for herself.

She hoped, too, as she finished drying off and slipping into her nightgown, that it was long enough for Damon to have settled down in the living-room and fallen asleep. She didn't want to have to face him again tonight.

He was asleep all right. On her bed.

Scowling, Kate crept towards the bed and peered down at him.

Damon was sprawled across it, face down, one arm outflung, the other tucked under his head. The khaki shorts and T-shirt he had been wearing lay in a heap on the floor. He was clad now in only a pair of light blue boxer shorts.

Kate stood quite still taking in the prospect of his smooth tanned back, the curve of his firmly muscled buttocks, the length of his hair-roughened legs. She'd always thought the Greek god business so much hot air. Now she wasn't so sure.

She closed her eyes and took a deep, steadying breath, then licked parched lips.

'Damon,' she said firmly. 'Get up.'

He didn't stir.

'Damon!' Her tone was louder and more irritable this time. She opened her eyes as she did so.

Still he didn't move.

Kate reached down and tugged on one of his feet. He groaned and pulled up his knee.

'Damon! Get up. It's time to go to bed.'

He made a muffled sound. ''m in bed.'

'It's my bed. My turn.'

'Share,' he mumbled into the sheet.

'No, I'm not going to share.' That way lay disaster. 'You're going to leave. Now.' Once more she reached for his foot and gave it a jerk.

A hand reached out and grasped hers, yanking her down on to the bed beside him.

'Oooff! Damon! Damn you!' She struggled against a surprisingly strong grip. 'Let go! Get up and get out of here. Now!'

'No. Too damn tired. Here——' he shoved over slightly '—your space.' His eyes fluttered shut again; his breathing deepened.

Kate wrenched her wrist out of his grasp and scrambled off the bed. She felt like punching him, like kicking him. Hard. She contented herself with smacking him once on the rear end.

He rolled on to his back and regarded her scowlingly from beneath hooded lids.

Kate stepped back hastily. 'You agreed. I took your word as a gentleman.'

'Your mistake.' A slight smile flickered across his mouth. 'You don't need to stand there with that look of outraged virtue on your face. I'm hardly any threat to you tonight. I can't keep my eyelids up, much less anything else.'

'Don't be crude.'

'I'm not being crude. I'm being accurate.' And he rolled over once more and started to snore.

Kate, hands on hips, glowered at him.

So, fine, he wasn't a gentleman. He was right about that. She should have known that from the first. A gentleman would never have proposed such a marriage!

Well, she certainly wasn't going to sleep in the same bed with him, then. How did she know he wasn't lying this time, too?

She should go straight up to the main house and sleep there. That would teach him. And it would certainly give Teresa something to call home about!

But even as she thought it, she knew she wouldn't. And not only for Damon's sake either. On her own behalf, she didn't want to disillusion Helena. She liked her new mother-in-law. She regretted that she was only going to have her a year. But as long as she did have her, Kate didn't want to see the worry and sadness she knew would appear on Damon's mother's face.

The more fool she, she thought grimly, echoing Damon's words.

Cursing both him and herself, she yanked the afghan off the back of the wicker chair and stalked into the living-room, shut out the lights and curled on the settee.

Half an hour of twisting this way and that convinced her she'd never get a moment's sleep if she stayed there. Grumbling, she placed the cushions on the wood floor and stretched out on them.

There, she thought, lying down, that was better.

Outside she could hear frogs croaking and insects chirping above the soft sound of the surf. Inside she could hear the bed creak as Damon rolled over. Her jaw tightened.

She turned on to her side, tucked the afghan around her, and willed herself to sleep. The moonlight bathed the room in a soft silvery glow. It was peaceful, she told herself. Soothing. She could sleep here. She knew she could. There was nothing to fear with Damon in the other room——

Except that dark shape scuttling across the floor towards her.

'Aargh!'

Kate leapt to her feet and scrambled to the chair, standing on it, her knees shaking, teeth chattering. 'God!' It was pure prayer, a desperate pleading for salvation. 'What the——' She unscrewed her tightly shut eyes and ventured a peek. It looked like the cockroach from hell. Used to the rather small, mundane New York City variety and hating them, she didn't even want to think about one the size of her fist.

Still trembling, Kate licked her lips. Another one appeared from beneath the cupboard.

She suppressed a squeak of horror, sinking on to the chair and wrapping her arms around her knees, clenching her teeth together to stop them from making noise. Her heart felt as if it were doing a fast-stepping dance in her chest. She took deep, even breaths, hoping it would slow down.

And all the while she gazed with morbid fascination as the two bugs trundled about the room, one of them moving towards the cushion she had just abandoned. She shuddered.

There was no way, *no way*, she was sleeping down there again tonight. Or ever.

Slowly, carefully, she relaxed her grip on her calves and stood up, still in the chair, still watching them unblinkingly as if one might suddenly decide to fly right at her.

Could they fly? It didn't bear thinking about.

She took a mighty leap and almost flew herself into the bedroom where she bounded into the bed next to Damon. He grunted as the bed jostled.

'I'm not sleeping out there! There are *bugs* out there!'

'Mmm.'

'You sleep out there!'

'No.' One arm reached out and slid around her shoulders, pulling her down firmly next to him.

'But——'

'Be quiet, Kate. Just be quiet and go to sleep.'

She tried wriggling out of his grasp, but he had her pinned beneath one strong arm and one hair-roughened leg.

''s me or the bugs, Kate,' he said sleepily. 'Take your pick.'

Some choice.

For what seemed like hours Kate lay, stiff as a board, as far towards her edge of the bed as possible while Damon made a soft whuffling sound, curled on his side and breathed more deeply.

At first she watched him expectantly, with as much trepidation as if he'd been one of those monster black bugs about to attack her. But time wore on and Damon didn't move.

Gradually she relaxed, felt the tension slip from her shoulders and her spine, felt her legs slacken and her fists unclench. But she didn't sleep. Couldn't.

She was too wide awake. Too aware.

Slowly, carefully, she turned on to her side so she could watch this man to whom she was married.

She remembered studying Damon briefly as he'd slept on the aeroplane, but that hadn't seemed nearly as intimate as this did. Then his features had softened slightly, his eyes had been closed, his collar button opened and his tie askew, but he'd still seemed remote and formidable in his starched white shirt and navy wool suit.

But as she lay beside him in bed, she found that he was formidable in an entirely different way now. It wasn't the hard-edged, decisive businessman that she felt in awe of this time, it was the supremely fit, well-muscled male.

And yet for all his masculine potential, she found herself feeling oddly protective of him.

Damon looked even more exhausted now than he had on the night flight back from Reno. The lines of fatigue on his face seemed more pronounced, the hollows of his eyes more deeply shadowed. And Kate found herself wanting to edge closer to him and put her arms around him, letting him rest his head against the softness of her breasts.

Oh, yes, right, and then what? she asked herself, irritated at her own foolishness. Would you really want what would happen next?

For there was no doubt in her mind that comforting would not be what would take place. He would want to make love.

Kate remembered the last time she had been in bed with a man, remembered the fiasco that had been her marriage — her *first* marriage, she corrected herself.

She had been eager and willing to make love with Bryce. At least, at first she had.

Of course she knew she was inexperienced; she hadn't thought it would matter. They loved each other, didn't they? So if things were awkward at first, it wouldn't matter. The expertise would come.

But Bryce didn't have the time or the patience for that.

He wanted his satisfaction and he wanted it now. Even that very first night he had reached for her rather impatiently and had taken as much satisfaction as he could get with her — 'not a lot,' he'd told her scornfully the day he'd left — then rolled away and fallen into a heavy slumber.

And Kate had lain awake at his side on their wedding-night feeling lonelier and less fulfilled than ever.

It hadn't got any better.

She cringed now at the memory of it. Worse, she recalled, she seemed to have been powerless to change it.

With Bryce the closeness she'd craved had always eluded her. They'd had sex, but they'd never had true intimacy, nothing like the soft words, gentle touches and implicit understanding that went beyond the body to touch the heart.

They hadn't had love.

Not really.

And in this marriage there was no love either.

For all that she was attracted to Damon, for all that she wanted to reach out to him, there was no use. No use pretending. Damon might awaken, he might reach for her, he might even consummate their marriage.

But he, too, would be simply assuaging a physical need.

And he would doubtless find her as lacking as Bryce apparently had. He would slake his need, use her the same way Bryce had, and he, too, would see the lack in her.

Kate couldn't even bear to think about it.

She'd loved once. She'd tried. She'd failed.

She didn't want — couldn't take — more of the same with Damon.

He awoke late. Restless and rested at the same time. The sun streamed in the window halfway up in the sky. Damon groaned. He could imagine what Teresa would say about that.

He could imagine what Kate would say too, for he realised that he was still lying in the bed. *Her* bed.

He remembered toppling on it last night, remembered listening to her turn on the shower, remembered telling himself that he'd move in a minute.

And then he remembered. . . What?

What did he remember? Some vague discussion with Kate. . .something about its being her bed, something about his being a gentleman. . .or not.

He groaned again.

Obviously he hadn't been.

And then? And then. . .

She'd left. And come back.

He rolled on to his back and rubbed his fists into his eyes, then pressed on them, trying to recapture the memory. Or had it been a dream?

He supposed it could have been a dream. He'd had enough of them lately. Lurid, erotic fantasies in which he and Kate had made slow, tantalising love.

This time he remembered—dreamed about?—reaching out in the night and finding her there. He'd been too tired to do more than draw her close and wrap his arms around her, then settle his chin in the curve of her shoulder and breathe in the sweetness of her hair.

He pulled the pillow over his face and folded his arms across it. He ached just thinking about it.

'Is this a new form of meditating or are you suffocating yourself?'

Damon jerked the pillow away from his face to see Kate at the foot of the bed looking down at him. He groped wildly for the sheet and was relieved to find that it covered him. Of course he was clothed—barely—but that didn't mean she wouldn't be able to notice his obvious arousal.

Hastily, still keeping the sheet over him, he sat up. 'How about trying to compose an apology?'

Kate cocked her head.

'I stole your bed.'

Was it his imagination or was she blushing? She took a quick step backwards.

'Yes, you did.' She avoided his gaze, going to open the blinds, then straightening the cloth on the small round table in front of the window.

He watched her, curious now, memories flitting in and out of his mind, teasing him, making him wonder. He traced a pattern in the sheet but his eyes never left her. 'So you slept on the floor?'

'Of course! You don't think I slept with you, do you?' Bright spots of colour stained her normally ivory cheeks.

'A man can hope.'

'Don't be ridiculous.'

'I have these memories, you see.' And he did even as he spoke. It was coming back to him now. 'Something about a bug. . .?'

Kate glared. 'Well, what did you expect me to do? Stay on the floor when there were insects the size of dinner plates waltzing around?'

'Ah.' He leaned back against the headboard and grinned up at her. 'So it wasn't a dream.'

'Some of it was! You were. . .you were. . .*snuggling*. . .up to me! Making noises!'

'Noises?' That wasn't the way he remembered it. 'Maybe I was kissing you.'

Her teeth came together. She lifted her chin and stared at the far corner of the ceiling and didn't reply.

'Was I?'

She stuffed her hands into the pockets of her shorts. 'Maybe you were.'

A corner of his mouth lifted wickedly. 'Couldn't you tell?'

Kate stamped her foot. 'All right, you were.'

'And obviously with great success. Did anyone ever tell you that you're terrific for a man's ego.'

'No one asked you to kiss me.'

'Was it disgusting?' He tried to sound as if it were purely a matter of idle curiosity. It wasn't. He wanted to kiss her again now that they were both awake. He wanted to grab her hand and pull her down on the bed beside him, strip off her shirt and smooth the shorts from her hips. He wanted. . .

Damn it! This was not the way to gain self-control and composure.

'I didn't come to talk about your kissing me,' Kate said stiffly. 'I came to tell you that Silas is up at the house. He wants to know if we want to go fishing.'

'Do we?'

Kate blinked. 'He said to ask you.'

'And I'm asking you. We are husband and wife on our honeymoon. We are spending the day together. Would you like to go fishing?'

She hesitated.

'What's the matter?' he asked.

'No one's ever asked me before.'

'To go fishing?'

'No. Well, that too, I guess. But what I meant was, no one's ever asked me whether I wanted to do something. My father, I mean. Or. . .or Bryce. They always just. . .assumed.'

He stared at her, amazed, and she shrugged helplessly, then ducked her head, the colour blooming in her cheeks again.

'It's not a big deal,' she said gruffly.

But Damon thought it was. He felt an unaccountable anger towards her father and her husband. What kind of men were they, not to take her wishes into consideration? 'Would you like to go fishing, Kate?'

She shot him an oblique glance as if to see if he meant it, and then gave a jerky nod. 'That would be nice.'

'And safer than kissing,' he said, needing to make her smile.

She looked startled, her eyes widening, her mouth making a silent O. Then she smiled, only a little at first, then more broadly as if they were co-conspirators again and not adversaries.

'Much safer,' she said and danced off towards the door. 'I'll tell Silas.'

* * *

Fishing. Yes, fishing was safe. Nothing could happen in a boat the size of Silas's. Especially with Silas in it, too, Kate told herself.

They moved from one fishing spot to another while Silas studied the reefs and the weather, which promised late day storms, muttered an occasional monosyllable and then nodded his head when he thought the fishing would be good.

Damon didn't dispute it. At first Kate found that surprising, expecting that as he was an expert in so many areas he would naturally assume he was an expert in this one. Heaven knew her father would have.

But Damon seemed content to let Silas do the leading today, only offering his expertise when it came to teaching her how to bait her hook. She felt all thumbs and more than a little foolish when she tried.

'I can't,' she said at first, pushing it away after she'd fumbled and dropped the piece of langousta Silas had offered her for bait.

'Here. Like this,' Damon said, and he was surprisingly patient as he showed her once more how to slip it on to the hook. 'Don't get so frantic. No one's grading you.'

Kate shot him a sceptical look, expecting sarcasm in his words, but he looked quite sincere and when he offered to demonstrate one more time, she nodded her head.

This time she got it, then cast the line overboard as Damon instructed her to. 'Now what?'

'Now we wait.'

If Kate had ever given much thought to fishing before, and she didn't remember having done so, she was fairly sure she would have thought it boring.

It wasn't.

It was soothing, centring. It gave a person time —

time to relax, to muse, to bask. All those things that fast-lane, big-city people like herself and Damon rarely had time for. And the miracle was, it could all be accomplished under the guise of actually doing something!

What a racket, she thought, smiling.

There was a sudden tug on her line and the reel began to spin. 'Oh!'

Damon grinned. 'Looks as if you've got a live one.'

The reel spun madly as she tried desperately to catch the whirling knob. At last she clamped down on it and stopped it. Then she thrust it towards Damon. He shook his head.

'It's your fish. Reel it in.'

It was harder than she'd imagined. This was no guppy on the end of her line, or if it was, they would be writing about it in Guinness. Her arms trembled from the exertion.

'You doin' good. Hang in there,' Silas encouraged her. 'Look there, he be comin'.'

Kate looked where he pointed and saw a silvery flash against the surface of the water, then felt the line jerk and she almost lost all the ground she'd gained. She bit down on her lip and tensed her fingers.

By the time she finally hauled him in, her arms were shaking, and she expected a fifty-pound barracuda to appear on the end of her line.

'A grouper,' Silas said as he netted the huge ugly yellowish fish. 'A baby.'

'A baby?' Kate croaked. 'Baby whale.'

Silas laughed, unhooking it and dropping it into the well. 'Naw. He be four, five pounds maybe at most.'

Kate stared.

'Bigger than mine,' Damon said, and Kate turned to note that while she'd been duelling with her grouper, Damon had landed a fish of his own.

'Yours is prettier,' she told him. It was a slim, shiny fish, much handsomer than hers.

'Thank you very much,' he replied, amusement in his tone. He grinned at her and Kate couldn't help responding in kind.

'Need some help baiting your hook this time?'

She shook her head. 'I'll try it on my own.'

It occurred to Kate then that Damon Alexakis wasn't very much like her father after all. Her father never would have bothered teaching her to bait the hook, nor would he have sat by and tolerated her clumsy attempts to follow his instructions. Neither would he have let her land it herself. He would have taken the whole project out of her hands and done it better.

He always did everything better. Including live other people's lives.

As she baited the hook, with less trouble this time, and cast, she thought about how, according to Teresa, Damon had spent the better part of yesterday dealing with his sisters' various complaints.

Eugene wouldn't have dealt with them.

'You made your bed, lie in it,' he would have told them, just as he'd told Kate when she married Bryce. And as long as she was married to Bryce, he'd never spoken to her. No matter how awful his sisters were, she couldn't imagine Damon turning his back on his family that way.

And that made her like him even more.

She didn't want to like Damon Alexakis. Being attracted to him was difficult enough. If she liked him as well. . .

Kate turned away from him, deliberately concentrating on Silas's strong calloused hands hauling in a hand line. But then Damon said, 'I've got another one,' and moments later he pulled in a shiny iridescent fish with frantic eyes and a gaping mouth.

Kate watched as it wriggled and twitched in the last throes of battle-weary panic fighting the man who'd caught it.

It reminded her of herself.

'I got to pick up some divers been to Doctor's Cay 'bout two o'clock,' Silas said after they'd fished for another couple of hours. 'You want to go home or —' here his grin widened '— you want to go to Rainbow Cove, do a little swimming, an' I pick you up later?'

'I don't have my suit,' Kate said doubtfully.

Silas grinned. 'Don't matter.'

Kate supposed it wouldn't. She could paddle around in her shorts and shirt perfectly well, and since the breeze had dropped she was feeling very hot and sticky.

'Let's go swimming,' Kate said impulsively. 'It would be so refreshing.'

Besides, they'd be gone from the house that much longer, away from the bedroom, out in the open where it was, as Damon had pointed out earlier, 'safer'.

'You tol' her 'bout Rainbow already, huh?' Silas nudged Damon.

'No, I didn't,' he said shortly. 'What about your sunburn, Kate?'

Kate shrugged. 'It's not bad. Please?'

'Such a willing woman.' Silas chuckled. Damon looked decidedly uncomfortable.

'What's it got, sharks?' Kate asked.

'No,' Damon said, and Silas laughed more heartily than ever. He opened the throttle and they surged away, heading north around the top of the mainland.

Rainbow was a secluded horseshoe-shaped cove entered by a narrow inlet. With a pristine pink sand beach tucked into a mangrove jungle, it looked like paradise. Kate was enchanted.

'It's beautiful, like a Garden of Eden.'

'You got that right.' Silas cut the engine and the boat slipped smoothly through the wave-less water towards the shore. 'You enjoy it, now,' he said as he helped her out in the shallow water. He winked at Damon and handed him some towels. 'I reckon I don't have to tell you that. Keep those clothes dry now.'

Then he opened the throttle and churned away.

'What'd he mean, keep our clothes dry?' Kate asked. 'How can you swim and keep your clothes. . .?' Her voice trailed off. Her eyes narrowed. She looked at Damon accusingly.

He scowled at her. 'Don't blame me. I wasn't the one who said, "let's", when he mentioned Rainbow Cove.'

'You didn't say it was the. . .the. . .'

'Skinny-dipping beach? It always has been.'

'How was I supposed to know that? You should have said no.'

'I'm supposed to say we can't go because it's a nude beach?'

'You didn't have to say *because* it's a nude beach. You could have. . .I don't know. . .you could have thought of something.'

'I did. Your sunburn.'

'Well, we don't have to,' she said after a moment.

'It's custom.'

'We'll break it.'

'Silas is a bigger gossip than any woman on this island. You think he won't tell? We're supposed to be newlyweds, damn it. I'd *want* to come here if this was a normal marriage!'

'Well, it's not, is it?' Kate said scathingly.

'No, it sure as hell isn't,' Damon said through gritted teeth.

'So swim if you want,' Kate said. 'I'll sit here until he comes back. Nice and dry, how's that?' She plopped herself down on the towel, brushed away a mosquito, and glared at him. 'I'll pretend I swam.'

'Maybe you can pretend your hair's wet, too.'

Kate picked up a handful of sand and threw it at him. 'Just shut up and swim. I'll close my eyes.'

'Don't do it on my account,' he said as his fingers went to the snap of his shorts.

She should have.

For a moment she did, shutting her eyes against the sight of his hands lowering the zip. But the temptation was too great, and her eyes flicked open again to watch as Damon slid the shorts down his hips and stepped out of them.

He was only the second male she'd seen totally nude. The first, of course, had been Bryce. But it took scant seconds for Kate to realise that Bryce naked was as different from Damon as it was possible for a man to be.

Blond and slim, Bryce had always looked suave and sophisticated in the three-piece suits he favoured. But whenever Kate had seen him undressed he had always seemed diminished somehow, lanky and hesitant, as if the clothes had indeed made the man.

The opposite was true of Damon.

If Damon Alexakis in a suit and tie had seemed to Kate the embodiment of masculine power, he was no less so stark naked. In fact, he was more.

Damon was lean without being lanky, firmly muscled without the least hint of fat. His chest was broad, his hips narrow, and his. . .well, his. . .Kate blushed and looked away, but not without having assertained that it was everything she might have expected.

'Little late to be checking out the merchandise, isn't it?'

'You said you didn't mind!' Kate muttered, her cheeks burning.

He grinned. 'I don't. Want to return the favour?' He stood right in front of her, looking down at her, still smiling and making no move to cover himself.

'No, I do not.'

'Spoilsport.'

'Just go swim.' Kate said to the sand.

'Sure you don't want to come along?'

'I'm fine.'

'Suit yourself, but you'll get awfully hot.'

He failed to mention that she would also get bitten by a million mosquitoes. She slapped one and then another, and another, and another. She jumped up and wrapped the towel around herself, swatting at the dive-bombing insects even as she did so. Damon, swimming away from her out in the middle of the cove, didn't notice.

'Drat!' She smacked her arm, getting two with one blow. But she couldn't even feel much satisfaction; three more took their places. She scowled fiercely, walked towards the trees in hope of some respite. But the insects were, if anything, worse there than they had been on the sand. She walked back towards the water.

Damon was perhaps forty yards out now, not really moving any longer, just floating, looking back at her. She slapped a mosquito on her leg, then another on her arm, then glared at him.

He smiled.

There was no breeze to speak of in the cove, either. Heavy dark clouds hung on the horizon, but they moved so slowly that Kate felt as if everything had stopped. She felt clammy, sticky, sweaty. Rivulets of perspiration ran down her neck, sliding along her spine, sticking between her breasts.

She glanced at her watch. Silas wouldn't be back for at least another two hours.

'Damn it,' she muttered under her breath, then out loud she called, 'Shut your eyes!'

'What?'

'You heard me, Alexakis. Damn it, shut them!'

He grinned. She couldn't tell if he shut them or not, he was too far away.

She wrapped a towel loosely around herself, then fumbled beneath it, unbuttoning her shirt. Then, holding the towel close, she slipped the shirt off. Her bra was sticking to her and she held the towel with her teeth while she wrestled it off. Then she wriggled out of her brief white shorts. She considered leaving her panties on. Silas would never know.

But the shorts she wore turned almost transparent when wet. A pair of wet panties under them would guarantee that the secret would be out.

Fuming, Kate peeled the panties off as well. She lay her clothes in a neat pile, Then with the towel still wrapped around her, she headed for the water.

'I think Silas is going to notice if the towels are wet, too,' Damon said from only twenty feet away.

Kate spun around. 'You're supposed to have your eyes closed.'

'It isn't as if I haven't seen a naked female before. I did grow up with six sisters.'

'And I suppose your sisters were the only ones you ever saw.'

'Well, there were maybe a few others.' He was smiling as he moved towards her.

'I'll bet. Stay where you are.'

Obediently Damon halted. 'I'm not the philanderer you seem to think I am.'

Kate wasn't going to argue with him. But she couldn't imagine Damon had spent much of his adult life as a practising celibate.

She was out past her knees when she knew she would have to get rid of the towel because she couldn't throw it any further. She cursed the gradual drop-off, but she had no choice. Whipping the towel towards the shore, she dived beneath the water in one fluid motion. She banged her nose on the shallow bottom and came up spluttering.

Damon stood a few feet away now, laughing.

'Wretch!' she cried, and flung herself at him, intending to drown him.

It was a major mistake.

CHAPTER SEVEN

'Ooof! Kate! Wai——'

But there was no waiting, no stopping. There was only fury, wild, unbridled frenzy, the product of a week and more of pent-up emotion, anguish, hunger.

Desire.

Of course, Kate didn't recognise that particular emotion at the moment of impact. All she wanted then was to throttle him, to choke his laughter, to wipe the mocking grin off his handsome devil's face.

But as satisfying as it was to knock him down, her own jolt was greater. He took her with him, grabbing her so that they both went under, their heads banging, their legs tangling, their bodies rubbing one against the other, inciting, exciting.

And when, at last, they righted themselves and stood, trembling, still touching, in waist-deep water, he didn't let her go.

'D-Damon.'

'Shh.' He drew her closer until her sea-slick body pressed once more against his, and then he bent his head and kissed her with a hunger that matched her own.

She knew she should be stopping him, pulling back, saying no. She didn't.

She couldn't.

She wanted it—she wanted *him*—too much.

She was wrong. She was foolish. She'd be sorry. She wasn't far enough gone to deny any of the above. And yet still she parted her lips under his and welcomed the touch of his tongue, meeting it with her own.

Perhaps it was because she'd been alone so long. Perhaps it was the pressure of propinquity, the temptation of this island paradise, a conspiracy of God, Greek mothers and mosquitoes. Kate didn't know.

She only knew she could fight no longer.

As his hands roved over her back and slid down to cup her buttocks, her own glided up the length of his arms and laced against the back of his neck. She rocked her hips forward into his. Then she felt herself being lifted and carried towards the shore.

He was as uncontrolled as she, as desperate, as hungry. He lay her down on the hard-packed sand at the water's edge and covered her body with his own, his damp hands stroking her with a fine tremor, his lips learning the line of her jaw, then touching her mouth again.

If there were mosquitoes then, she didn't notice them. If there was sand in her hair, she didn't care. The only thing that mattered was this terrible need that had been building for as long as she could remember.

And the only place to assuage it seemed to be in Damon's arms.

He pulled back for a brief moment to settle himself between her legs and even that fleeting separation found her reaching for him, drawing him down once again.

Damon didn't argue. He came to her, crushing her into the sand, biting down on his lower lip as he reached the centre of her, shuddering as he stopped, held perfectly still, his eyes locking with hers.

It was insanity. Madness.

It was the most beautiful thing on earth.

Love.

Or if it wasn't love, it was the closest thing Kate had

ever known, the closest she'd come to feeling favoured, cherished, beloved in her entire life.

For Damon was nothing like Bryce had been. Bryce had been so perfunctory, so mechanical and sometimes so obviously elsewhere that she'd despaired of reaching him. There was nothing like that about Damon. He was so clearly eager for her that Kate found herself coming to meet him, lifting her hips to draw him further within, arching her back so that her breasts brushed against his chest, digging her fingers into his hard-muscled buttocks, making him lose control.

'Oh, Kate! I can't — I need — ' His thrusts became quicker, stronger.

Kate's did, too, because something else was happening, something new, something powerful. She forgot Bryce, forgot the past, forgot everything but Damon. Her own movements became more abandoned, her body more responsive to the delicious friction growing between them. And then as he tensed and his muscles contracted, the same thing happened to her own.

It was as if she was still in the water, being lifted and lifted and lifted by the surge of the ocean's power, and then, at the peak, she felt herself slip over and fall headlong into the rush of the wave. It was liberating, shattering, mind-boggling.

It had never happened before.

Kate shut her eyes and delighted in it, revelling in sensations, in the feelings, in the weight of the body lying on top of her own. Her heart slammed against the wall of her chest. She turned her head and her lips brushed a faintly stubbled cheek.

She drew back and opened her eyes to meet Damon's brown ones. And then the crush of reality weighed more heavily than her husband's body.

She held her breath, waiting for him to roll away, to leave her the way Bryce always had, or — worse — to tell her, as Bryce had, exactly how disappointed he was, how unresponsive she was, how little she met his needs.

But though Damon did move off of her, he didn't leave. Instead he settled himself in the sand alongside her, their bodies still touching, one of his hands stroking lightly down the length of her. She felt his fingers tremble.

'Well,' he said after a moment, giving her a faint grin, 'that was worth waiting for.' And the husky, ragged tone of his voice made her pull back, startled.

'What do you mean?' she said cautiously.

'Do you suppose it was the frustration that did it?' he mused, still smiling. 'Or is it the chemistry between us? I think we ought to find out, don't you.'

And before Kate realised what was happening, it was happening again!

Damon's hands skimmed over her, learning her curves and hollows. His mouth explored her breasts, laving them leisurely, suckling deeply, setting off tremors within her. She arched her back, clutching at him, moaning.

'You like that, do you?' he whispered. 'Me, too.'

But then he pulled back and instinctively Kate reached for him. Then she looked up from beneath heavy lids to see him positioning himself above her once more.

He settled himself between her thighs, urging her legs to part for him. And they did, flexing and lifting so that her heels pressed against the back of his thighs as he slid into her.

'Yes,' Kate murmured, 'oh, yes.' Because this was the way she knew loving was supposed to feel. This was the connectedness she'd always hoped for, that she'd sought with Bryce and never found. 'Oh, my love, yes.'

And then she felt the hot surge of his seed within her, felt her own body contract around him and her mind explode at the climax of her desire. She shut her eyes. Her heart hammered, then gradually slowed. Her muscles relaxed and she began to hear again the soft beat of the rippling waves against their bodies, the cry of the gull overhead, the whisper of the wind through the palms.

Slowly, with considerable trepidation, she opened her eyes. Damon still lay on top of her, but he had braced his torso with his hands alongside her arms, and he was looking down at her, his expression unreadable.

Tentatively Kate smiled.

And Damon smiled back. He levered himself up and off her. 'Amazing.'

And Kate's smile broadened because, yes, it had been.

Damon got to his feet and held out his hand to her. When she took it, he pulled her up beside him. Then, lacing his fingers together with hers, he led her into the water.

It was more than Eden, Kate thought. It was heaven—the warm clear water and the soft blue sky. It didn't even feel as warm now. Or maybe, she acknowledged, that was because the heat of frustration and anger no longer tormented her. She was basking in the glow of fulfilment.

She supposed she ought to be worrying. She'd made love with a man who had never said, 'I love you'. She'd shared her most intimate self with a man who was going to be gone in less than a year.

And yet she couldn't regret it. She tried. She couldn't. It had been too beautiful. Too fulfilling. Too wonderful to second-guess or to wish it had never happened.

She slanted a sidelong glance at this man who was for twelve short months to be her husband, and she couldn't help thinking, yes, this is the way it's supposed to be. This is the point at which two souls connect.

And what if she never came closer than this? What if for the rest of her life she was destined to miss such connections? Wasn't it better to have experienced it once?

Was she a sinner to have enjoyed it? To have found with Damon's help a part of herself that no man, certainly not Bryce, had ever touched?

No, Kate decided, she was not. They were married, for however long or short a time. They had a right to the happiness they could find.

And after?

But Kate knew better than to ask the answer to that. She knew better than to count on happily ever after. She'd done that once to her everlasting regret.

For now it was enough to live in the moment. And to share with Damon that most elemental connection that two human beings can share.

She studied her husband's unyielding profile. Her eyes traced the hard lines of his face, unsoftened now by his dark wavy hair which was plastered wetly to his skull. He was, she thought, even more handsome than usual, more striking, more vitally masculine. Damon Alexakis was the essence of what was truly male.

And for the first time in her life, in Damon's embrace, Kate felt as if she'd touched that essence.

Who'd have believed it?

Damon sat silently in the stern of Silas's boat and studied the woman he'd married less than three weeks ago. Whoever would have thought there was all that passion, all the eagerness buttoned up inside the proper, professional Kate McKee?

Not me, that's for sure, Damon thought now.

And yet. . .

And yet, hadn't she attracted him almost from the first? Hadn't he wanted to touch her ivory skin, kiss her delectable mouth, ruffle that shiny, silky brown hair?

His hormones had known, Damon thought wryly, even if his rational mind hadn't.

And his hormones were pleased. He couldn't help grinning. And when Silas looked at him and muttered about newlyweds, then shook his head, Damon laughed aloud.

Kate turned and caught them both looking at her. Beneath her already sunburned cheeks he saw a hint of deepening colour. But when they continued smiling at her, she began, albeit shyly, to smile, too.

And when she did, he wanted her again.

He'd thought an afternoon's loving would do it. He'd expected that learning her mysteries would quench his desire. In fact, what he'd learned had only whetted his appetite for more.

She'd been so responsive, so abandoned, when he'd touched her. And afterwards she'd seemed almost astonished by it all. Hadn't her husband made her feel like that? Damon wondered.

Then he thought, of course he had. She wouldn't have loved him so much if he'd left her unsatisfied in bed. What Damon had tapped in her was, quite obviously, a well of long-denied yearning.

Maybe she hadn't loved a man since her husband's death. It hadn't taken long for him to realise that she clearly hadn't been interested in Stephanos.

Maybe he was the first to have touched her in four long years. Of course she'd have exploded like match-struck kindling, if she hadn't known intimacy in all that time. Of course she'd have been eager.

He wanted to strike a match to her desire again. And again.

'You look like you done got the catch of the century,' Teresa said when she saw them coming up the walk. He had his arm around Kate, had done since they'd left the village, and she hadn't pulled away. 'You be smilin' big.' Teresa smiled even bigger in demonstration. 'Or maybe,' she said, cocking her head, 'you got other things make you happy.'

'Maybe,' Damon agreed.

Kate stepped on his foot and nudged him in the ribs. He grinned at her, but he didn't let go. 'Silas is bringing the fish up when he cleans them,' he told Teresa, 'We got a box fish.'

Teresa nodded, pleased. 'That be almost cause for those smiles. I'll stuff it for dinner.'

'We'll be here around seven,' Damon said, leading Kate towards the cottage.

This morning he'd hated the cottage. Had spent the first part of their time fishing, trying to contrive a means to stay out of it for as long as possible. It had seemed like the cage containing all his frustrations.

Now he wanted to lock the two of them in and throw away the key. He wanted all the privacy the honeymoon cottage would allow.

He knew that getting to make love to Kate was more than he'd bargained for. He could scarcely believe his good luck. It was turning into a far better honeymoon than he'd had any right to expect. She could make the year they had to spend together a hell of a lot more pleasant than he'd anticipated it being.

'You can have the shower first,' she said to him as he opened the door.

'You don't think we might share?'

If he'd thought her face turned red before, it was nothing compared to the colour it turned now.

'I don't—I mean, I've never—' She stopped and turned away, pressing her palms to her cheeks in dismay.

Charmed, Damon turned and drew her into his arms. 'You've never been that wanton, huh?' he said, smiling.

She shook her head against his chest. He was unaccountably pleased: at least she hadn't been there before with Bryce.

'Scared?'

She lifted her eyes and shot him a quick glance before ducking her head again. 'Don't be silly,' she said gruffly.

'Come on,' he said, tugging her with him towards the bath, 'let's give it a try.'

She didn't protest. She allowed him to lead her into the bathroom, and she leaned against the door while Damon turned on the shower and adjusted the temperature of the water and the angle of the spray. He flicked a bit of water at her. 'Warm enough?'

She nodded. She didn't say a word. He pulled his T-shirt over his head, then turned to her.

'Waiting for me to do it?' he asked softly.

She swallowed. 'N-not really.' She started to lift her own shirt, but he put out his hands and stilled hers.

'I want to.'

Slowly, carefully, he slid his hands under the hem of her shirt and skimmed it upwards. His thumbs brushed against her silky midriff, then skated lightly across her nipples. Gathering the shirt as he went, he tugged it over her head, then dropped it at their feet.

Kate didn't move. Damon lay his hands on her arms, slid them down and then up, stroking her warm flesh. She trembled under his touch.

'Cold?'

'N-no. Burning,' she admitted.

So was he. 'You can touch me, too, you know.'

For a moment Damon didn't think she would. She looked at him, her eyes wide and slightly wary as she hesitated. Then she licked her lips quickly and brought her hands up and lay them against his chest.

Her touch made him tremble. He swallowed, holding quite still as her fingers traced lightly on his chest, then lifted to touch his shoulders and skim down the length of his arms. Her fingers laced with his. Then she leaned forward and touched her lips to his chest, laving first one tiny hard nipple, then the other.

Damon let out an explosive breath.

'Don't you like that?'

'Hell, yes, I like it! Too much. I'm going to——' He shook his head desperately.

She smiled. It was a wanton smile, a teasing smile, a very definite 'come hither' smile. And Damon had no inclination to resist. He loosed his fingers from hers, reaching out to undo the fastening of her shorts and pull down the zip. They fell to the floor, pooling at her feet.

Kate stepped away from them. She started kissing him again, her lips feathering across his chest and lightly brushing his shoulders, while her palms flattened against his abdomen. Then they stroked downwards and hooked inside the waistband of his shorts.

Damon held his breath as the backs of her fingers caressed his taut belly, then tugged his shorts down past his hips. He kicked them off and drew Kate with him into the shower.

Her skin felt soft and slick and wet as he wrapped his arms around her and nuzzled against her neck. She made a tiny, hungry, whimpering sound that sent a fierce shaft of desire surging through him. He could have taken her then in scant seconds. Deliberately he did not.

He was no randy teenager in the mood for a quick fix. He was a man grown, a man willing and able to appreciate the finer things in life. And making love with a woman as warm and responsive as Kate was definitely one of them.

He stepped back, reached for the soap and, taking deep, calming breaths, tried to concentrate strictly on the satiny texture of her flesh as he smoothed the soap over her shoulders and down her back. Closing his eyes, he let his fingers stir up a lather, then slide forward to wash her small, but perfect breasts. They were faintly pink from being bared to the sun, and his fingers trembled as he moved the soap in gentle circles on them.

Kate trembled, too. She stood very still, but he could feel the tremors running through her. And he smiled to see her lean into the stroke of his hands. He slid the soap lower, still circling as he moved to her abdomen. Bending his head, he kissed each of her breasts in turn.

She reached out and gripped his shoulders with surprising force, her nails digging into his back. He left a trail of hot kisses down her belly until he reached the top of the soft triangle of dark hair at the apex of her thighs. His hands continued stroking down her legs. First the left, then the right, down the front of her thighs, then up the back. Around to the front again and down. He let the soap fall to the floor of the shower.

Then slowly his hands slid between her knees and he let his fingers move upwards, brushing lightly, stroking gently. Kate shifted, widening her stance. Damon smiled, pleased.

He rested his forehead against her abdomen, watching as he slowly let his fingers creep further up the tanned length of her legs until they reached the soft petals of flesh that hid her secrets from him. And then he touched her and felt her fingers let go of his shoulders only to clench frantically in his hair.

'Damon!'

He lifted his face and smiled up at her, his fingers stroking her all the while, finding her wet and welcoming, trembling themselves at her readiness to receive him. Her legs quivered and her hips surged against his hands.

'Damon! What are you doing to me!'

'Giving you pleasure.'

'Yes, but you ——'

'Don't worry. I'll get mine,' he promised. It was pleasure enough watching her, seeing a Kate he'd only just discovered — a wild, passionate Kate who burst into flames at his touch.

She was close to doing so now. He could see it in her face, could feel it in the movements of her body, in the eager thrust of her hips against his hand. Her fingers twisted in his hair, tugging it, pulling him up.

And he came up willingly, lifting her as he did so. She wrapped her legs around his hips as he pressed her against the wall and slid into her welcoming warmth.

As much as he would have liked to prolong it, he couldn't. The feel of her body around his overwhelmed him, and he moved with an eagerness that matched hers. He was only relieved that he brought her satisfaction before succumbing to his own.

'H-heavens,' Kate mumbled as he let her body slide down his until her feet touched the floor again. 'Good grief. I've never ——' She glanced up at him, then looked away, apparently embarrassed. She bent over and snagged the bar of soap.

Damon kissed the nape of her neck, then leaned

against the wall of the shower, his legs still trembling. 'Me neither,' he said.

Kate shot him a quick look. 'Really?'

'Really,' he answered mockingly.

She blushed. 'You liked it?' she asked almost hesitantly.

Damon stared. 'What do you think?' He wrapped her in his arms and gave her a wet, soapy hug. 'So much that if I didn't think it would kill me, I'd do it again right now.'

Kate beamed.

She couldn't believe she was acting this way. She was like some wanton woman who couldn't keep her hands off a man. Not just any man. Damon Alexakis.

And of course, she couldn't discuss the way she felt with anyone. They'd stare at her as if she'd lost her mind. Why shouldn't she want him? they'd ask. Why shouldn't she *have* him? After all, he was her husband.

'In name only,' she said aloud now in the still darkness of night.

Really? she replied. Who was she trying to kid?

They'd made love again that evening after dinner, hardly able to wait, barely enjoying the box fish and conch salad Teresa had prepared. They were too eager for the taste of each other. And though she knew she ought to be trying to control her desire, nothing in Kate seemed to want to rein it in.

It was too new, too astonishing. She was like a child with a new toy — an amazing, unanticipated toy. And she couldn't get enough of it.

Of him.

She was, to her everlasting chagrin, wanton and embarrassed by her wantonness at the same time.

It was her insatiable need to be close to Damon that had forced her from the bed in the middle of the night.

She awoke to find herself snuggling against his back, wrapping her arms around him, touching him in places that would have shocked her less than twenty-four hours before.

She knew that she could awaken him, rouse him, make the world spin for both of them again. And at the same time she didn't dare. She didn't want to want him this badly. She didn't want to give in to the temptation to make love with him once more.

It was too marvellous, too exciting, too passionate.

It scared her. *She* scared herself. What had become of the steady, reliable, no-nonsense woman she'd been for the past twenty-odd years, especially for the past four? Of course she'd dreamed of finding such an all-consuming love, but she'd expected to find it with Bryce, with a man she loved.

'At least,' she told her reflection in the mirror, 'you found it with the man you married.'

For a year.

'A lot can happen in a year,' she went on determinedly.

And you think he's going to fall in love with you?

Did she?

She pressed her palms against her cheeks, staring at her reflection, as her mind delicately probed the notion of Damon Alexakis loving her.

Twenty-four hours ago she'd have laughed at the idea. Now she wasn't sure. She only knew that in the space of a day they had connected on a very basic level, on a level she'd never come close to with another man, even Bryce.

Damon had pleasured her, just as he'd said he was pleasured. But he'd done more than that. He'd taught her things about herself that she'd never even suspected. He'd shared himself in a way that Bryce never had. He'd made her aware of her potential as a woman.

She shut out the light in the bathroom and crept quietly back to the bed. In the silver moonlight Damon lay sprawled, the sheet draped loosely over his hips. His dark hair was mussed and spiky, his cheeks and jaw shadowed with a day's worth of beard. Kate eased herself down on the bed beside him, feasting her eyes, remembering the way his hands had moved over her, recalling the tension in his face as he had loved her, and the fierce possession when he'd made her his own.

She'd left the bed so she wouldn't be tempted to touch him. It was no use. She stroked a lock of hair off his forehead, smiling at his restless response, at the way his hand groped, seeking hers.

His eyes opened. 'Kate?'

'I'm sorry. I was restless. I didn't mean to disturb you.'

He smiled, a lazy, slumbrous smile. 'Didn't you?' And he drew her down into his arms once more, his hands tracing her curves, exploring her hollows, making her shiver and begin again to burn.

'I'm not sure a week is long enough,' he said against her lips.

'What do you mean? Long enough for what?'

'A honeymoon. I think we ought to stick around, really convince my mother.' He smiled into her eyes. His hands were melting her. 'What do you say?'

'Yes.'

CHAPTER EIGHT

IT TURNED into a beautiful honeymoon.

They had a beautiful island, gorgeous weather, a private cottage, and the occasional smiling approval of Teresa.

They'd had all that from the first, of course. But then all it had done was frustrate them, highlighting exactly what they were missing: each other.

When they came together at last, the equation became complete.

Teresa obviously noticed. As she was cleaning up after supper the following day, she gave them a big grin. 'You two lookin' better. I think maybe this marriage be gonna work.'

'You've given it your stamp of approval, have you?' Damon said to her, but he was looking at Kate.

'Hard not to, lookin' at the two of you. You lookin' like the cat that ate the hen, and the hen lookin' like she enjoyed every minute.'

Damon laughed and Kate blushed furiously.

'Your mama goin' to be so pleased,' Teresa went on. 'She can't hardly wait to come, she that happy you're going to stay on for the holiday.'

He had told Teresa they would be staying on over the holiday when they'd come for breakfast that morning, and she had obviously wasted no time in passing the word on to the rest of the family.

'Your mama say Mr Stephanos and Mrs Sophia stay in the big house. You get to keep the cottage.'

Damon smiled at her, but spared a wicked one for Kate as well. 'You'd better believe it.'

Teresa chuckled at the renewed flush on Kate's face.

'You don't have to be quite so blatant,' she muttered once Teresa had departed.

Damon's gaze was one of guileless innocence. 'About what?' Then he laughed and rubbed his ankle where she kicked him. 'You're beautiful when you blush,' he told her.

Kate made a face. 'Thanks very much.'

'I mean it, Kate.' His expression sobered.

Kate swallowed at the heat she saw in his eyes. 'You've been celibate too long,' she said gruffly. 'You'd think anyone was appealing who satisfied you.'

'Is that what you think?'

'This is a marriage of convenience, isn't it? And I'm ever so convenient.' She shot him a defiant look.

Damon didn't reply. He pushed back the chair and stood up. Kate's gaze followed him warily. He looked taller and more powerful than ever this morning. He held out his hand to her. She hesitated. Then, when he kept holding it out, waiting, she put her own in it. His fingers closed around hers and he pulled her to her feet.

More convenience? she wondered, but she didn't dare ask. There was something dangerous in his expression, something she didn't completely understand, and wasn't sure she wanted to.

But what else could it be? she asked herself. And really, she wasn't objecting. Making love with Damon under whatever circumstances was amazing.

She was surprised when they got back to the cottage that he didn't haul her into the bedroom. He said only, 'Get your suit and let's go for a swim.'

After they'd changed, they went down to the beach. Damon was quiet, and Kate, still unsure of his mood, but aware that something had changed, kept her mouth shut as well.

She wondered if she had hurt his feelings somehow, implying that any woman would have done. But she didn't see how that could have hurt him.

It was more likely to hurt her, which was, if she was honest, why she'd said it. She didn't want to let herself believe it was as wonderful for Damon as it was for her. If she did, she might start hoping. . .

And that would be disaster.

Damon walked down the beach without speaking until they reached a tall sculpture made of the flotsam and jetsam that had washed up on the pink sand.

Kate hadn't walked this way before and until they'd come close she hadn't even realised what the sculpture was made of. Now she stood looking at it, awed at the vision that had created beauty out of scrap. Damon seemed in no hurry to move on, and she ventured to ask. 'Who made it?'

'Whoever came by. It was started before we first came here. Even if it gets washed away in a storm, someone starts it again.'

'It's beautiful.'

'You think so?'

Kate glanced at him, surprised. 'Yes. Don't you?'

He nodded. 'But it doesn't appeal to everyone. Not enough structure.'

'Its spontaneity is what makes it beautiful, and its ability to take whatever comes to hand and make it work.'

Damon didn't say anything, and Kate wondered if she'd made another mistake. Then he took his towel from around his neck and asked, 'Do you want to swim?'

'Here?'

'There's a good reef out there.' He pointed, then shrugged. 'But if you'd rather not. . .'

'It's fine,' Kate said quickly. 'I'm getting hot.'

A corner of his mouth quirked. 'Are you?'

She felt her cheeks begin to warm. 'Not that kind of hot,' she said quickly.

'More's the pity,' Damon drawled. He dropped his towel and walked towards the water. When he reached the edge, he turned around. 'Come on, then.'

Whatever had been bothering him seemed to fade as they waded into the water and began to swim. He helped her fit on a snorkel and fins, then fitted on his own and led her out to swim over the reef. It was even more beautiful than the sculpture, and Kate told him so.

'I thought you might like it.' He smiled at her. She smiled back, and suddenly the day seemed bright again.

He didn't let her stay out too long. 'Too much sun at midday,' he told her. And she went with him willingly back to the cottage.

This time he did lead her into the bedroom. And after another shower together, they shared the bed for a nap and an afternoon of quiet loving.

Damon Alexakis quietly attentive was as awesome as Damon fiery and passionate had been. There were so many sides to him, so much to find out that she didn't know, that Kate lay awake watching him sleep, marvelling at the man she was married to, trying to decide what it was about him that fascinated her so.

What she decided was that there was no one thing. There wasn't simply the smooth, polished charm that she'd been taken in by with Bryce. Damon had charm, of course. He had charm in spades. But besides the charm, he had strength, passion, gentleness, humour, determination, vulnerability. More things than she could count.

If she'd guessed there was all this to the man who'd

proposed to her those few short weeks ago, would she have dared to say yes?

'It's a miracle,' Sophia said.

'It is,' Electra echoed.

'The eighth wonder of the modern world,' Pandora affirmed. 'I'd never have believed it if I hadn't seen it.'

'What are you talking about?' Kate asked her sisters-in-law. They were all sitting under beach umbrellas, sipping long, cool drinks while Damon taught his nieces how to swim in the shallow water before them.

'That,' Sophia said, nodding towards her brother and her daughters. Damon was crouching low in the water, Christina hanging on his shoulders while he helped Leda keep her legs straight as she kicked.

'That's it! You're getting it! Good job,' he praised.

'He tried to drown me,' Electra recalled.

Kate laughed. 'You're kidding.'

'I am not!'

'Maybe you deserved it,' Kate said with a small grin, remembering how trying Damon sometimes found his sisters.

Electra looked offended, then chagrined. 'Maybe,' she allowed.

'You were sort of a pain,' Chloe chipped in. 'But I think it's a miracle anyway.'

'Actually,' Sophia said, 'it's Kate.'

Kate glanced at her, startled. 'You mean, it's because of me that Damon is paying attention to the girls? Nonsense. He took them out before we were married.'

'He took them out when he was courting you. Before that I think he came to their birthday parties with gifts picked by the corporate buyer at F.A.O. Schwarz. He certainly never taught them how to swim. Nor did he read them bedtime stories.'

'Well, perhaps that was my fault,' Kate allowed. 'I was reading to them last night and he. . .dropped by.'

'He's in love,' said Chloe.

'Deep.' Pandora.

'And he wants to be a daddy.' Electra.

'Amazing,' Sophia said, shaking her head yet again.

Kate wanted to protest. She didn't dare. What was she going to say? That her husband wasn't in love with her, certainly not deeply so. And he didn't want children at all from her. He only wanted sex.

She wished she could dig a hole and bury herself. Instead she jumped to her feet. 'I need a swim,' she said and strode quickly down the beach and plunged into the water, heading out past Damon and the girls without even stoppng, though Leda shouted,

'Hey, Auntie Kate, lookit me swim!' and Christina said,

'Can I come with you, Auntie Kate?' and Damon said,

'Where are you going?'

She didn't answer, just plunged beneath the incoming wave and stroked straight ahead. She needed coolness, she needed space, she needed time to think.

Damon's head popped up next to hers. 'What's going on?'

'I thought you were teaching the girls to swim.'

'I took a break. They don't have long attention-spans.' He winked. 'You taught me that.'

She had, damn it. She'd said it only last night that a short book was better than a long one with them. She'd wanted to get back to the cottage with Damon and make love. She knew he remembered, that he was thinking about it now.

'Well, I'm sure they can use a little more than you've given them,' Kate said, turning and swimming away.

Damon followed her. 'They'll get their turn. Is

something bothering you? Are my sisters hassling you?'

'What do you care?' Kate said sourly.

He reached out and caught her arm, stopping her easily. She scrabbled for a toehold on the ocean floor, but it was too deep, and she started to sink.

'Damon!'

He hauled her against him, keeping her head above water. 'There. Got you. Relax.'

'How'm I supposed to relax like this?' She was plastered against him, could feel the slip of his thigh between her legs and the hard press of his chest against her breasts.

'You did a pretty good job of it last night,' he said into her ear, then kissed it, nibbling lightly on the lobe. A shiver ran through her.

'Damon! Stop it! They're watching!'

'So?' He kissed her again, this time trailing light kisses along her jaw, then taking her mouth with even more thoroughness. She gripped his shoulders and tried to pull away. He held her fast. An unbroken wave surged past them, lifting them together, rubbing their bodies one against the other, and Kate could feel the evidence of his desire. She shut her eyes, remembering how he had looked last night, naked and aroused.

'What did they say, Kate?'

'W-who?' She shook her head, trying to think straight. It wasn't easy. 'Oh, you mean your sisters? Th-they're amazed. They think you're in love with me.' She gave a weak half-laugh. 'You've really got them convinced.'

'Have I?' There was a note of strain in Damon's voice.

'Yes.' She gave him a shove and was delighted to

find that he let her go. 'You really have,' she added tightly.

'And you don't like that?'

She tried to shrug it off. 'It's what we'd hoped for, certainly. And. . .we do have most of the year left so I suppose they have to think something.'

'I suppose they do,' Damon said quietly after a moment. He was treading water now, staying next to her, but not touching her. Kate felt better, more in control.

'So,' she said lightly, 'I guess it's all right. For the time being.'

'Of course.' He paused. 'And after, Kate?'

'After?'

'After Thanksgiving. When we're home again. What do you want them to think?'

She managed as carefree a smile as she could. 'Oh, I don't care. I guess we can see what happens, can't we?' She allowed her gaze to meet his only for the briefest of moments. She was afraid he might see that their marriage was beginning to matter to her — that *he* was beginning to matter.

But she wasn't sure how to feel when he gave her a small, lopsided smile. 'I guess we can.'

What the hell had he expected from her? A declaration of undying love?

Yeah, right, Alexakis. Damon had been arguing with himself all the way down the beach, running as if the hounds of hell were after him. 'Working out' he'd told his mother. 'Going for a quick jog,' he'd told Stephanos. *Trying to make some sense out of the mess he'd been making of his life*.

Probably, he thought as his feet pounded along the hard-packed sand, he shouldn't have suggested staying for Thanksgiving week. Lord knew why he had.

Well, actually he knew, too. He'd done it because he hadn't wanted to go back. He and Kate had connected that day at Rainbow. They'd had the most marvellous sex he'd ever experienced in his life.

He'd only guessed that sex like that existed. Probably he'd listened to his sisters long enough to have some sort of imprint on the back of his mind that convinced him there could be more to sex than the simple physical satisfaction that he got from playing a good hard game of racquet ball or having a quickie with his most recent girlfriend.

But he hadn't really known for sure — until Kate.

And then he'd thought it was a fluke. A once-in-a-million type thing. Except now it had happened eight times out of eight, and he was looking for chances to make it happen again.

And there was more.

He liked her.

He liked to talk with her. She was witty and well-read. She listened to him, then offered her own views. And she wasn't hesitant about disagreeing with him if she felt he was wrong.

'Don't you know you're not supposed to argue with your husband?' he'd teased her last night after the family supper and she'd taken exception to his view on a recent book they'd both read.

'Don't you know you love it when I do?' she'd countered. And they'd both stopped dead, flushing deeply, when they'd realised the truth of what she said.

'And now one of you had better haul the other off to the cottage and show each other just how much,' Pandora drawled, and all the sisters giggled, while the nieces looked confused and Stephanos looked at Damon and Kate intently.

Helena's knitting needles clicked complacently as

she smiled at her son and new daughter-in-law. 'I told you so,' she'd said.

Damon's feet pounded harder now, trying to blot the memory out of his head.

Why?

Why did he care?

It was what he wanted, wasn't it? To make his mother think he'd fallen in love? To make sure he had the freedom to pick his own bride in his own time?

Hell, how long ago had Kate pointed out to him that that reason was no longer valid?

God, he was confused!

He stumbled and crashed down on to the sand, his heart hammering like an anvil in his chest, his ears pounding, the blood roaring in his veins. And all he could think was that the last time his heart had hammered and his ears had pounded and his blood had roared, he'd been making love with Kate.

'Where were you?'

'Out.'

'What were you doing?'

'Thinking.'

'About. . .us?'

'What else?'

She was sitting in the bed, a lacy white cotton nightgown barely covering her breasts, her glossy dark hair freshly washed and curling damply against her head. She looked cool and self-possessed and absolutely delectable.

He groaned.

'What's wrong?'

He gave her a wry look. 'Pulled a muscle.' He hooked his thumbs in the waistband of his shorts and peeled them down, kicking them off and moving towards the bathroom as he did so.

He went in and shut the door, then flipped the shower on to cold. For a moment he stood braced with his hands on the white marble countertop and hung his head, breathing hard, fighting his desire. He had to be able to control it if he was ever going to control what he felt about her. He had to be able to walk past her and not want her, had to be able to look at her and see a business associate, not a woman he wanted.

The door opened.

He looked around. 'What do you want?'

His tone was rough enough to make her hesitate. Then she gave him a hopeful smile. 'I thought I'd help.'

She was already moving past him, sticking her hand under the tap, shuddering at the icy spray. She turned it down and turned on the hot, adjusting the temperature, putting the plug into the bottom of the tub.

'What the hell are you doing?'

'Running you a bath.'

'I want a shower.' A cold one, he thought desperately.

But Kate ignored him, opening the taps full force so that warm vapour from the water soon fogged the mirror and began to fill the room. Then she turned to him and waited.

'I'll wash your back.'

'Swell,' he grumbled. But he got into the tub and sank down into the water, wishing that it didn't feel so good, wishing that she'd just go away.

'You'll enjoy it,' she promised.

'That's what I'm afraid of,' he muttered.

Kate cocked her head. 'Why?' Her blue eyes were wide and curious.

Damon's jaw tightened. 'Never mind.'

'Are you afraid you're falling for me?' Did she sound as if she hoped he was? Like hell. She didn't give a damn as long as she got her passion, her climaxes, all the sex she'd missed since her hot-blooded husband had died.

He snorted and was surprised to see a flicker of hurt in her eyes. Did she care?

He didn't know what to say. He handed her a washcloth. 'Since you're here, maybe you should make yourself useful,' he said gruffly.

The hurt, if that was indeed what it had been, vanished. She took the cloth. 'Whatever you say.'

He shouldn't have encouraged her, though God knew she needed no encouragement. She was all too happy to run her hands over him, to soap his shoulders and his back, to let the washcloth drift slowly back and forth across his chest, then move lower still.

'Kate,' he muttered through clenched teeth.

'Mm hm?' She was sitting beside the tub on the floor, smiling at him, her gaze slumbrous and enticing as she moved the washcloth over him.

'You're going to get it if you keep that up.'

Her smile widened as she touched him. 'I'm not keeping it up Damon. You are.'

He surged up out of the water, reaching for her at the same time.

'Damon!' She scrambled out of his way, then grabbed a towel and came back towards him. 'You should have let me finish washing you.'

He lifted a brow. 'Was that what you were doing?'

She blushed. It made her look young and innocent. But she wasn't, damn it. He knew that. 'Did you do it to Bryce?' he demanded before he could help himself.

She flinched, then looked away. 'This has nothing to do with Bryce!'

The hell it didn't. Everything he did with her in bed had to do with Bryce. It was like having a ghost there with them. He scowled and grabbed the towel from her, drying himself off.

'It doesn't, Damon,' she insisted. 'Really.'

He wiped his face, looking at her over the top of the towel. She was looking at him with a sort of urgent sincerity that made him begin to believe her. 'It doesn't?'

'No.' She turned away then somewhat hastily and went out of the bathroom, shutting the door behind her.

Didn't it? Damon asked himself, staring at the door between them. Didn't it?

Then did it have to do with him?

And if it did?

He felt a combination of panic and confusion. He felt lost and hopeful. He finished drying off, then toweled his hair as well, before opening the door.

The light was off, but in the glow from the bathroom light he could see that she was in bed, lying on her side, facing away from him. He shut off the light and crossed the room to stand next to the bed on the side away from her. For a long moment he debated going into the living-room and trying another night on the settee.

He couldn't.

He pulled back the sheet and slipped into bed beside her. Touched her arm. 'Kate?'

She didn't move, but he heard her swallow.

With his hand he stroked her bare flesh and felt again the quickening of his desire. He edged closer. 'Kate? Come to me. Please.' He turned her, unresisting in his arms and drew her close, kissed her cheeks, her shoulders, her lips. 'I want you.'

And Kate stifled her worries and her fears and her better judgement because, heaven help her, she wanted him, too.

* * *

She wanted him.

Oh, yes. And that would have been bad enough, but there was more. She began to realise it when they were back in New York, back to his work and hers, to the pursuit of their daily lives.

She loved him.

She wasn't sure exactly when it began, when the uninterest turned to interest, when the interest turned to liking, when the liking turned to love. She only began to realise gradually that it had.

Her feelings had begun, she supposed, even before they left — that last night on the island, when she and Damon and all his family had been in the big house. Pandora had been playing the piano and Daphne the guitar. They'd been singing — everything from Greek folk tunes to Lennon and McCartney favourites — and when she'd returned from the kitchen with a cup of tea for Damon's mother, he had reached out and snagged her hand, pulling her down into his lap, where he held her close in his arms.

And Kate had let him. She'd come willingly, and she'd realised as she did so that she wasn't doing it to show his family that she loved him, she wasn't doing it out of some need to perpetuate a fiction, she was doing it because it was where she wanted to be.

Just as she wanted to be a part of the Alexakis tribe. That had become increasingly apparent to her, too. They were the family she'd never had — the laughing, squabbling siblings she'd longed for, the fussing mother she'd missed, the husband who made her feel warm and cherished and beloved.

Maybe he was only doing it because he was acting. She couldn't tell any more. Sometimes she thought so. Sometimes she thought he was beginning to care for her as much as she was learning to care for him.

And every night now when she crossed the days off

the calendar, she did it with less conviction, with more anguish, and she knew she no longer looked forward to the end of their year together.

She wasn't sure how Damon felt. He didn't bury himself in his work the minute they got back to New York. He came home early some nights, picking her up at Sophia's to take her out to dinner. Now and then he suggested taking the girls with them to give Sophia and Stephanos a break. And those nights were wonderful, too. They gave Kate an even greater sense of what Damon would be like as a father. He would be great.

Most nights, however, he brought her straight home. Sometimes he encouraged Mrs Vincent to take the evening off and he helped Kate cook dinner. Afterwards, as they did the washing-up, he asked her how her day went, listened to her problems, shared some of his own, then he took her to bed and loved her with a passion and a thoroughness that Kate had at first been unable to believe existed, and now knew she couldn't live without.

Thanksgiving became a wonderful memory. Christmas was right around the corner. They were, in spite of their beginning, in spite of their intent, making a marriage together.

And as the holiday approached, Kate smiled every day. She blossomed under Damon's watchful eye.

Most of all, she hoped.

CHAPTER NINE

'ARE you sure you'll be all right if I go to East Hampton tomorrow for the weekend?' Kate asked her sister-in-law, who was sitting placidly on the sofa next to the window overlooking Central Park. She wanted Sophia to say no.

Sophia gave an airy wave. 'Of course. *I'll* be fine. Mama is surprisingly helpful, really. Damon isn't going to be happy, though.'

Kate hoped she was right. Damon didn't know about her proposed trip to East Hampton. He'd still been at a late-night board meeting when it had come up, and when he had got home there had been far more interesting things to occupy them!

Anyway, she'd hoped that a quick glance through her files would find her the replacement nanny she needed and she wouldn't have to go at all.

No such luck. And the Barlowes, early and valued clients, deserved a perfect stand-in for their beloved Charlotte who'd broken her leg on a skiing holiday. No, the only thing for it was to go out there and see to things herself, then find the right woman to fill in.

Unless Damon said no. She hoped that he would object. She hoped he would tell her in no uncertain terms that she wasn't going anywhere five days before Christmas, that she belonged at home with him.

But for the time being, 'It's my job,' she reminded Sophia.

'I don't understand why you persist in doing it. Good heavens, it isn't as if Damon can't afford to support you!'

'I need to do it. For me.' Which was as close as she dared come to explaining that there might be a time when Damon would no longer be supporting her.

Their marriage was working out far better than she'd ever dared hope, but so far she'd never ventured a word about extending it, making it permanent, and Damon hadn't either. She had fallen in love, but she didn't know that he had. He liked her, he liked the sex they shared. Beyond that. . .Kate hoped. She dreamed. She was afraid to ask.

Maybe when she told him she had to leave, he would say something. Maybe he would give her some hint about how he felt.

'You're going to miss the Christmas party!' Sophia remembered suddenly. She looked at Kate, stricken.

Kate had already realised that. The Alexakis Enterprises Christmas party had been the topic of much conversation recently. Though Greeks traditionally celebrated Christmas at the feast of Epiphany in January, the Alexakises had, ever since Aristotle had begun the main US branch many years ago, taken this opportunity to share the joys of the season with all the people with whom they did business. Kate remembered Damon saying his father had never met a holiday he hadn't had a use for. She smiled.

But, as much as it had begun as a purely business event, it had grown to become a family occasion, too. And this year was to be the first they'd all attended in five years.

Recently one sister or another had been missing each year. Once Damon's mother hadn't been able to come. Three years ago Damon himself had had an unavoidable conflict and had been unable to make it. But even though they might not always get there, they always tried.

It had to do with being there for one another, being a part of the family. Sophia had explained it to her. So had Helena. And Pandora. And Daphne.

That was perhaps why, Kate thought, her proposed trip to East Hampton might prompt him to share some indication of how he felt. Would he care if she missed the party? Did he really want her to be part of his family? Or was she no more than a playmate who happened to be his wife?

'Damon won't let you miss it,' Sophia said positively now.

Kate gave a little shrug and tried not to let Sophia see how she felt.

'You'll see,' Sophia promised.

Kate didn't because, ultimately, she didn't see Damon.

He called when she had gone to take the girls skating at Wollman Rink.

'He said he's flying to Montreal,' Sophia told her disgustedly when she and the girls returned. 'Some crisis or other. It was Stephanos's account actually, but Damon didn't think Stephanos should go right now. Because of the baby being almost due,' she added apologetically.

'I understand,' Kate said. She did. And she shouldn't be disappointed. She wasn't a child, after all. She was an adult. She should know by now she had to make her own decisions. And anyway, Damon wasn't letting their marriage stop him going places. 'Did he say when he'd be back?'

Sophia shook her head. 'Like everything else, it depends.'

Kate managed a wan smile, knowing how true that was. There were a thousand vagaries connected with exports and imports. Weather. Shipping schedules.

Trade agreements. It wasn't surprising, and it was, of course, the right thing for Damon to do.

She had better do the same.

'You'll stay here tonight, then, won't you? Mama will be alone with the girls while Stephanos and I go to a play. She'd love to have you, and there's no sense in going home if Damon's not there.'

No, there wasn't. It would be lonely as anything rattling around the big apartment alone. But Kate didn't really want to stay at Sophia's either. With Helena alone this evening, there would be lots of conversation, lots of dissembling, lots of worry that she might say the wrong thing. Kate still felt guilty about deceiving her mother-in-law.

'I think,' she told Sophia, 'that I'll head on out to East Hampton.'

He went to the party straight from the airport. So what if he wasn't wearing the dinner-jacket still hanging in the closet in the apartment? Who cared that his trouser cuffs were wet from the new snow? What difference did it make if he didn't stop to shave? Why worry about what all the dealers and company reps thought?

None of it mattered — as long as he could be with Kate.

Damon wasn't quite sure when he'd begun to realise that. Maybe it had begun to crystallise when he'd found out that Stephanos had fouled up yet another account and the only way to settle it was to go to Montreal and take charge. He hadn't wanted to go.

It was a first.

Ordinarily, troubleshooting was what Damon liked most. He sometimes thought he relished his brother-in-law's screw-ups because they gave him a chance to do what he did best: rush to the rescue and save the day.

This time he'd wanted to send Stephanos.

He couldn't.

Sophia was due the first week in January, slightly less than three weeks away. Damon didn't necessarily imagine that she would go into labour the moment Stephanos left the country, but his sister was high-strung, the baby was active, and Sophia had already had several occasions of false labour pains.

He considered sending Arete, then rejected it. Tension between Arete and Stephanos was already high. Each of them continually vied to be considered Damon's second-in-command. It would only make things worse if he allowed his sister to step into Stephanos's territory.

So if they weren't going to lose the account, Damon would have to go himself.

And that was when he'd thought of taking Kate along.

Would she go? He'd thought she might. She didn't seem to be able to get enough of him. And he damn sure couldn't get enough of her, he'd thought, smiling as he'd dialled Sophia's number.

But Kate had been out with the girls. They wouldn't be back until right before supper, Sophia told him.

Hell, he'd thought. Damn. So much for snatching her away and taking her with him.

'Tell her I have to go to Montreal,' Damon had said.

He'd tried to call her later when he'd got to Montreal. She wasn't home. Neither was Mrs Vincent these days. He and Kate had given her weekends off and she usually went to visit her daughter in Philadelphia.

He'd called back to Sophia's, but only his mother was there. She didn't know where Kate was.

He tried again for the rest of the evening between

meetings with Monsieur Belliard. The only voice he
heard was his own on the answering machine.

It had been past midnight when he got back to his
hotel room. He'd tried one last time, got nothing and
dialled Sophia again.

Stephanos had answered. 'What's wrong?'

'Where's Kate?'

'Damned if I know,' Stephanos had grumbled
sleepily.

'Ask Sophia.'

'She's sleeping.'

'Wake her up.'

'Not on your life! She gets little enough sleep these
days with that baby, and I'm —— '

'Wake her up!'

Stephanos did. He came back a few moments later.
'Kate's in East Hampton. Business, Sophia says. Now
go to sleep.' He hung up.

So did Damon. He didn't sleep.

He lay awake missing her, thinking about the way
she curled so comfortably into his body, about the
silky smoothness of her skin, the soft luxuriance of her
hair, the little moans and gasps of pleasure she made
when he loved her.

It was the first night he'd spent without her since
he'd come back from Paris. It was the first time he'd
slept alone since they'd made theirs a real marriage.

Was it a real marriage, then?

The question caught him by surprise.

Did he want it to be? Did he want to love and
honour and cherish Kate for the rest of his life?
Did he want to take the vows he'd made as a business proposition and turn them into a lifetime
commitment?

Did she?

He was on the phone to Sophia at the crack of dawn.

'Where in East Hampton is she?'

'I haven't a clue,' Sophia said sleepily. 'Don't fret. You ran out on her first.'

'I didn't run out on her!' Damon almost shouted.

'Whatever. Can I go back to sleep now? I need my rest, Damon. You'll understand better when you have children.'

Something else he hadn't thought about. He swallowed. 'Yeah. I've got one long meeting this afternoon with Belliard, then I'll be home. Tell her.'

It hadn't been his most successful rescue attempt, but he'd managed to do a fairly creditable job. It was over, that was what counted. He shook hands with Belliard, caught a taxi, cursed the snowstorm blanketing the east, bullied his way through the Christmas crowds at the airport. First class tickets, usually no problem to come by, were at a premium due to the holiday. Economy had long since been sold out.

'We're doing the best we can, Mr Alexakis,' the counter attendant assured him. 'The snow is slowing us down and everyone wants to get home for Christmas.'

Not the way he did, Damon had thought, and was sure that God was on his side when an hour later there was a vacant seat. He made it to LaGuardia, caught another taxi. This one slipped and slid its way through the snow directly to the posh East Side hotel where the party was already in progress.

He didn't stop until he set foot inside the festively decorated room. And then his eyes searched the premises for Kate.

Arete appeared out of nowhere and took his arm, drawing him with her as she spoke. 'You might've shaved, and why didn't you change? Well, at least you're back. Just in time to charm Mrs Fredericks, too.' She steered him towards the wife of one of their main shipping contractors.

'Where's Kate?' Damon demanded.

Arete shrugged. 'How should I know?'

'Have you seen her?'

'No. But I haven't looked.' She turned him forcibly and shoved him in the direction of Martha Fredericks. 'Charm,' she commanded.

He did his best, all the while scanning the crowd for the sight of his wife. He thought he saw her once near Sophia. But then the woman turned his way and he saw that he was wrong.

'. . .hear you got married recently,' Martha Fredericks was saying. 'Love to meet her. Like to get a glimpse of the woman who brought you down.'

Had she, Damon wondered, brought him down? Was that what had happened to him? He still couldn't find her. Mrs Fredericks rabbited on. He smiled vaguely, spotted Pandora and another woman coming their way and reached out to grab them. He'd been charming. It was their turn.

'Tell Mrs Fredericks about your trip to Italy,' he commanded his sister.

Pandora, who had been smiling, looked as if she was about to burst into tears, and Damon suddenly remembered why she'd gone to Italy, with whom, and that the skunk had dumped her when her money ran out.

'Sorry,' he muttered. 'I mean, tell her about the Knicks game you went to.'

Pandora didn't look particularly mollified, but she shrugged. 'Sure. And you can get Eleni a glass of champagne. You remember Eleni, don't you?'

The woman with her, she meant. And yes, now that he looked at this Eleni, he did remember her vaguely. A tall, striking young woman with thick dark hair and lustrous brown eyes. A beauty, certainly. He remembered her as something less.

'You were a—uh—school friend of Pan's?'

Eleni smiled. 'I was. She used to bring me home sometimes for holidays. You know my father, Nikos Vassilakis.'

'Of course. How is he?'

He led Eleni over to the table and snagged two glasses of champagne, not really listening as she talked about her father, his business, his hopes for the future. He still hadn't found Kate.

Hadn't she come back yet?

Finally he dumped Eleni on Electra and asked once again for his wife. 'Ask Sophia,' Electra advised.

His sister was holding court on an elegant white silk sofa that Arete had arranged for her. Stephanos was, thankfully, hovering over her, making sure she was comfortable, making sure she was protected from jostling and cigarette smoke, being the sort of husband he should have been all along.

'Where's Kate? Isn't she back?' Damon asked his sister.

Sophia gave him a sympathetic look and shook her head. 'I'm sorry.'

Damon was, too. He sagged down on to the sofa next to her. Why had he hurried? Why had he busted himself to get here? What difference did it make?

None, obviously, as far as Kate was concerned.

Kate opened the door quietly, unsure what to expect, knowing what she wanted to find but fearful just the same. She'd spent the entire day yesterday with the Barlowes, had got a feel for their children, and had realised that the best possible interim replacement would be Ellie Partridge, the sixtyish lady she had in mind for Sophia after the baby was born. Her own replacement.

Ellie had, bless her heart, been willing to come. In fact, at Kate's urging, she'd caught a late train out from Manhattan and had arrived last night. But by the time Kate had introduced her to the family, it was too late to head back to the city herself.

Early this morning, however, Ned Barlowe had got up and taken her to the station. She'd fidgeted and fussed, her mind totally consumed by Damon, day-dreaming about him all the way home.

She wasn't sure he'd even got back yet. But in the best of all possible worlds, he would be waiting for her when she came in. He would open sleepy eyes and smile at her, reach for her and pull her into bed with him, making love to her with the passion she relished. And she would love him. Then he would tell her that he'd missed her, that he loved her, that he wanted their marriage to last forever.

And that would be as good as or even better than his not wanting her to go to East Hampton in the first place.

She hung her coat in the cupboard, slipped off her shoes and padded down the hall towards the bedroom. Her pace quickened when she heard water running in the master bathroom. She reached the door, then slowed, wondering what his reaction would be.

The door to the bathroom was slightly ajar and she could see Damon's back as he stood facing the mirror. He wore a pair of dark wool trousers, but nothing else, and as Kate watched him shave she could see the muscles flex in his back. She felt a quickening inside her, a need to touch him, to run her hands over that smooth bronzed skin. She moved forward, wanting to go to him and put her arms around him.

He either heard her or caught a glimpse of her in

the mirror for quite suddenly, he turned, the razor still in his hand, one side of his face still lathered.

'You got back,' she said and smiled, walking towards him. 'When?'

'Last night.' His tone was even. He didn't smile. He didn't act loverlike at all.

Kate stopped. 'Oh,' she said brightly. 'Then. . .you got to the party after all?'

'I was the host,' he reminded her shortly.

'But you had to go to Montreal. I thought Sophia and Stephanos. . .' But what did it matter, really, who was the host? He had been there and she hadn't. 'I-I'm sorry. I wanted to be there. But I had this crisis come up. The Barlowes——'

'Don't worry about it.' He turned and went back to shaving, concentrating on his reflection, ignoring her.

Kate watched him, dismayed. She felt shut out, frantic. She swallowed and bit her lip. 'I missed you,' she offered after a moment.

Damon made a non-commital sound and kept on shaving. 'You had work to do,' he said after a moment, excusing her. And it didn't sound as if he cared at all.

Kate felt her throat tighten. She stepped back into the bedroom. 'Shall I—shall I fix us some breakfast?'

He shook his head. 'I've eaten. I have to get to the office.'

'It's Sunday.'

'I have work to do.'

And, fifteen minutes later, he left. He didn't even come into the kitchen to say goodbye. She heard the door shut and, by the time she ran to open it the lift door was sliding shut and he was gone.

Kate closed the door and slowly dragged herself back to the kitchen. Last night's storms had disappeared, leaving a cloudless blue sky. Bright winter light still shone in the wide glass, but it seemed to Kate as if a cloud had blotted the sun.

After breakfast she went to Sophia's. She didn't want to be alone and, even though she knew that going to Sophia's would get her more deeply involved with the family, she told herself that Sophia would appreciate help with the girls.

Sophia was, in fact, delighted. 'They're driving me crazy,' she admitted. 'They're getting so excited about the holiday. They were allowed to attend the first half-hour of the party last night. It was supposed to mollify them. I think it was a mistake.'

'If I'd been there I could have kept them away,' Kate said.

'No, if you'd been there, Damon would have monopolised you.' Sophia smiled.

Kate doubted that. He hadn't seemed to care at all. She wondered if he'd even noticed she was gone. 'Would you like me to take the girls to the park for a while?'

'Would you? Just for an hour or so.' Sophia yawned. 'The baby didn't give me any rest last night.'

Sophia retired to her bedroom while Kate bundled the girls into their jackets and mittens. The door to the study opened as they were leaving. Stephanos smiled at them.

'You're back,' he said to Kate, and he seemed more pleased to see her than Damon had.

'Kate's going to take us skating again, Papa,' Leda told him. 'Can you come, too?'

'Please, Papa,' begged Christina.

'Girls, your father has plenty of work to do,' Kate said quickly, but Stephanos shrugged.

'Why not?'

Kate opened her mouth to protest, then realised she couldn't. Not in front of the girls. Stephanos seemed to know what she'd been going to say, though, for he gave her a brief smile.

'Don't worry,' he told her, 'I've learned my lesson.'

'What lesson, Papa?' Christina demanded.

Stephanos shrugged into his jacket and opened the door for them. 'It's not important, little one,' he said gently. 'Let's go.'

The girls were delighted to have their father along. And as they walked to the park, Kate felt less self-conscious and apprehensive in his presence as well. Stephanos had come a long way from the lecherous man who'd sought a nanny and something more. Damon had been right: he'd never made a move on her again. In fact, over the past couple of months Kate had seen him grow increasingly more doting when it came to Sophia. And now his interest seemed to extend to the girls as well.

He helped them lace up their skates, then stood back and watched, a proud father expression on his face, as they let go of his hands and skated away. 'Amazing,' he said after a moment. 'One minute they're babies, the next they're off to school. I missed a lot of it.'

Kate didn't say anything, just stood watching the girls. Privately she agreed, but she didn't imagine he wanted to hear it.

'I owe it to you, waking me up,' he said. 'You and Damon.'

Then she did look at him. 'What?'

He had the grace to look embarrassed. 'Watching you two fall in love made me take another look at Sophia. At what I'd had with her — and was in danger of losing.'

Kate could feel her own cheeks warm. She looked away, not wanting Stephanos to see the guilt on her face.

'I'm not saying this to embarrass you,' he told her. 'I'm trying to say thanks.'

'You're welcome,' she mumbled.

'When I married Sophia, I was in love with her. Desperately in love. I'd have done anything for her. Including going to work in her family business, which was what she wanted. Including always coming in second to Damon.'

Kate shot him an oblique glance, interested in what he was saying, edging closer, still however, keeping most of her visible attention on the girls.

'I don't like admitting it, but it began to get on my nerves. Everything I did, everything I tried, it seemed as if the whole family thought Damon could have done better. I got mad. And——' he raked a hand through his hair '—I started staying away. Going out on my own. Finding my own friends. What the hell? I thought. What do they care? I figured I was a disappointment to Sophia.'

'She never said that to me,' Kate told him quickly. 'I think she loves you very much.'

'I do, too,' Stephanos admitted. 'But it took you to make me see it.' He dug his toe in the newly fallen snow. 'I thought Damon was only marrying you to make sure I kept my hands off. I thought, good, serves him right, getting in a marriage like that, him so bound and determined to do everything right. And then I saw that he really loved you.'

Kate blinked. 'You did? When?'

'Everywhere. Right from the first. The way he looked at you. How attentive he was. How he didn't let you out of his sight on the island.'

Sex, Kate told herself. It was because he valued her physically. But somewhere deep inside she felt a shaft of hope.

'And if you'd seen him last night when you weren't there.'

'What happened last night?'

'He came rushing in late straight from the plane from Montreal. He didn't even change. And he wanted to know where you were.'

'And that shows how much he loves me?' Kate knew she might be betraying her doubts to Stephanos, but she couldn't help it. She needed to know what he knew.

'If he didn't, he'd have been drooling all over Eleni.'

'Who's Eleni?'

'A friend of Pan's. Gorgeous woman. Her father was a colleague of Mr Alexakis. Eleni's got a business of her own now—something in textiles—but Pan says she'd give it up in a minute if the right man came along.'

'Damon?'

Stephanos scowled at her. 'Of course not. He's married to you. Oops, there goes Leda, right on her nose!' And Stephanos took off across the ice rink to rescue his daughter.

Damon loved her.

Kate wished she could believe it. With all her heart and all her soul, she wished that the man she loved loved her.

Sometimes, like in the middle of the night when he turned to her in passion or in the middle of Christmas afternoon when he walked behind her chair and brushed a hand across her hair, she could almost believe he did.

Or maybe then she was just better able to fool herself. For certainly other times he seemed preoccupied, distracted, as if he really wasn't a part of her world at all.

Still, Kate was loath to believe otherwise as long as she had a chance.

And she thought she did, until the day that Nestor Stephanos Adropolis made his appearance in the world.

It was the day after New Year's. Sophia had awakened before dawn with a faint backache. She hadn't wanted to bother anyone, she told the family later, so she'd waited until the vague ache had escalated into contractions five minutes apart. Then she woke her husband.

'You have to come now! Now!' Stephanos was frantic when Kate picked up the bedside phone.

'I'll be right there.'

'Tell him to relax,' Damon said loud enough for his brother-in-law to hear.

'I'll tell him that when you're having your first,' Stephanos said roughly to Kate. 'Get over here now.'

'We will,' Kate promised in her best soothing voice and hung up. 'Come on. It's time.'

Sophia, for all that she began her labour quickly, got most of the way there, then slowed down. Kate, at home with the girls, waited by the phone for what seemed like hours until, at last, the call came at five that evening.

'It's a boy,' Stephanos told her, and he sounded exhausted enough to have given birth himself.

'Congratulations,' Kate said. 'How's Sophia?'

'Tired. Fine, but tired. We both are. We'd thought about having you bring the girls up tonight to see him, but I think it would be better if you wait until tomorrow.'

'Of course,' Kate agreed, though she was eager to see the baby herself.

'Damon will bring you the Polaroids.'

'He was there?'

'Waiting in the hall the whole time. You didn't imagine he'd let the next generation arrive without him, did you?' Stephanos teased.

'No,' Kate said. 'Of course not.'

Stephanos was right, of course. The baby would matter a lot to Damon. As much as he might grumble about his mother and his sisters and their problems, he was always right there to solve them or at least to lend moral support. Kate had often thought about what a good father he would be. She tried to imagine a child they might have, then stopped. It was far too tempting.

Damon came bearing Polaroids and Chinese take-away. The girls were so excited to see photos of their new brother that they only picked at the sweet and sour pork. It took Damon's most determined stern-father look to get them to settle down and eat.

'You won't be able to go see him tomorrow,' he told his nieces, 'if you don't eat a good dinner and get plenty of sleep tonight.'

The girls calmed down enough to eat. After an hour of television and three bedtime stories, they allowed the light to go out. Eventually they even slept, leaving Damon and Kate alone together.

For days it seemed they'd done nothing much more than pass in hallways and chat inconsequentially over meals. There'd been nights of passion, of course, but the closeness Kate had sensed building between them seemed to be eluding them now.

She told herself that it would pass. She knew Damon had a lot on his mind with the problems in Montreal, and she knew more work than ever was falling on his shoulders, especially since Stephanos was preoccupied with his wife and new arrival.

But ever since her conversation at the ice rink with her brother-in-law, Kate had told herself that it would work out, that she had reason to hope.

Damon loved her.

Now she came back into the living-room to find Damon concentrating on a magazine. 'He's lovely, isn't he?' she asked, carrying the pictures as she came back from checking on the girls.

Damon glanced up briefly. 'Wrinkled and red, actually.' His dismissive tone surprised her.

She laughed. 'All babies are. They improve.'

Damon shrugged. 'Good thing.' He went back to his magazine as if it were far more interesting than she was.

Deliberately Kate sat down on the sofa next to him, edging close, hoping he would put his arm around her and draw her into an embrace, hoping that Nestor's birth would spark a paternal instinct in Damon, would make him want sons of his own — with her.

He stiffened slightly, then stood up and rubbed a hand against the back of his neck, leaving her alone on the couch. 'I've got work to do,' he muttered. 'All those hours at the hospital. . .'

He didn't even look at her, just crossed the room and grabbed his briefcase which was still by the front door. 'I'll use Stephanos's study.'

When Stephanos came home about ten he was still there. Kate listened to her brother-in-law, bubbling and eager to talk about his new son. She smiled, praised, said all the right things. Then she went to bed in the guest-room where she and Damon had agreed to spend the night.

Damon was still working.

It was past midnight when he came in, but she hadn't slept; she'd thought. And she was still thinking as she watched him strip off his clothes in the dark and slip into bed beside her.

'Damon?' she touched his arm.

He tensed for an instant, then turned to her, took

her into his arms and kissed her. It was a hungry kiss. Almost, Kate would have said, a desperate kiss.

And then he loved her, shattered her. . .and then he slept.

She saw Nestor Stephanos the next afternoon. He was wrinkly and red and very, very beautiful. Simply seeing him made her ache with maternal longings. She sat beside Sophia's bed and held him in her arms and cooed down at him, marvelling at the way his dark eyes tried to focus on her, at the way his tiny hand gripped her finger so fiercely. She looked over at Sophia and smiled.

'He's gorgeous!'

Kate looked up to see Helena, Pandora and a dark-haired woman she didn't know standing in the door-way. Behind them, looking at her, was Damon. He ushered them in as Helena looked at the unknown woman with grandmotherly disdain.

'Of course he is, Eleni,' she said. 'How could you possibly think otherwise?'

The dark-haired woman, obviously the Eleni that Stephanos had mentioned, laughed and crossed the room to stand by Kate and smile down at her and the baby. 'May I?'

Reluctantly Kate gave him up, watching as the other woman cuddled the baby close. 'Isn't he precious?' Eleni asked. 'Don't you wish you had one of your own, Damon?' She slanted a glance at her friend's brother.

And Kate, looking at Damon, saw an expression on his face that she'd never seen before: a wistfulness, a hunger that sent a shaft of yearning right through her.

And then he looked at her and something happened. The wistfulness faded, the hunger died. His expression closed. He shrugged.

She couldn't lie to herself any longer. She couldn't pretend that their marriage would ever be more than the sham Damon had offered her at the first.

No matter what she'd begun to hope, they had a marriage of convenience, nothing else.

The passion, the sex, the joy they'd taken in each other's bodies was physical release and nothing more. Of course he'd taken her when she'd been willing. He was a man, wasn't he? Men were quite willing to share sex without love.

And, despite what Stephanos had claimed, he didn't love her.

If he did, he wouldn't withdraw from her. He would talk to her, share with her, confide in her. He wouldn't brush her off and walk away.

He wouldn't pretend uninterest in children when it was clear he wanted some of his own.

What was even more clear was that he didn't want them with her.

Did he want them with Eleni?

Kate didn't know. Maybe. Maybe not. Certainly he'd looked enchanted at the sight of Eleni holding the baby.

But it really didn't matter whether it was Eleni or some other woman that he some day fell in love with. It only mattered that he didn't love her.

It was cowardly, and she knew it, but she couldn't live the lie any longer. She waited three days, until the Barlowes' nanny Charlotte was back on her feet and able to cope. Then she called Mrs Partridge back from East Hampton and settled her in with Sophia, the twins and a far less red and wrinkled Nestor. It was nothing more or less than what she'd intended to do all along, she told them — and herself.

She kissed the baby and hugged the girls. She smiled. She waved.

'You're not leaving forever,' Sophia said. 'You're only going home to Damon.'

Kate smiled again as she backed out of the door and blinked back the tears. She did go home to Damon's, but only long enough to leave him a note.

Then she packed her bags and left.

CHAPTER TEN

SHE was gone.

He couldn't believe it. No, that wasn't true. He believed it; he just didn't want to.

The pain was terrifying. The hollowness he felt went almost beyond bearing. And even telling himself that he'd expected it didn't help at all.

Because, no matter how much he'd got the feeling since she'd come back from East Hampton that he was losing her, he'd told himself she wouldn't really go.

And when he'd come into Sophia's hospital room and had seen Kate sitting in the chair, holding the baby in her arms, he'd felt they might really have a chance. She'd looked so beautiful, so content. And when Eleni had taken the baby from her, she'd seemed bereft.

And he'd imagined giving her a child of her own. *Their* own. A child who would cement the bonds that had begun to form between them, a child who would give them an excuse for prolonging their marriage, for making it a forever proposition.

Even when he'd looked at Eleni holding his nephew, in his mind's eye he'd still seen Kate, had envisaged her cuddling their own child like that, then looking up at him as if he'd made her universe complete.

And then she was gone.

No warning. No discussion. Nothing but a terse little note.

I think we've done this long enough. I can't lie any longer. Regards, Kate.

Regards. *Regards*! As if they were no more than acquaintances, fleeting ones at that.

Maybe we are, Damon thought wearily. She'd been gone a week. He hadn't heard a word. She didn't love him. That was obvious. He had been enough for her in bed, taking the place of dear departed Bryce while the lights were low. But in the long run he'd never had a chance. When she'd seen the baby, when she'd realised what she was missing, the physical relationship she'd had with Damon had paled. She hadn't been able to lie about what she really wanted. And a family with Damon wasn't it.

He poured himself another drink — one of the many too many he'd had since she'd left. Then he flung himself down on the sofa and stared through blurred eyes at the ceiling.

In his hand he held a small calendar he'd found in the drawer of the bedside table. Kate's calendar. With the days marked off one by one since the day she'd married him.

How long would she have kept marking? The question was rhetorical. He knew the answer without asking — until at last she was free of him.

His throat ached and tightened; his head throbbed.

He was supposed to go to a meeting at three with Belliard. The old man had flown down from Montreal to finalise the deal. Damon didn't care. He should have been at the office hours ago. He'd never missed a day in sixteen years. Until now.

Now he'd missed a week. Four days, really, but even when he'd gone to work, he hadn't been there.

'What's the matter with you?' Arete had demanded more times than he could count. 'You aren't listening to a thing I've said.'

'What do you mean, you don't know where the

Belliard file is,' Stephanos asked him. 'You're the one who had it.'

'Damon, are you sick?'

'Damon, is there something wrong with Kate?'

'Damon, you can't go on like this.'

It had taken four days and considerable harassment from Stephanos and Sophia for him to even admit what was wrong.

'What do you mean, she's left you?' Sophia demanded, horrified. 'What did you do to her, Damon?'

Damon couldn't answer that. He'd simply sat in their parlour, staring at the scotch in his hands and shaken his head.

Sophia quickly changed her tack. 'She'll be back,' she prophesied. 'She's probably just having some post-honeymoon jitters.'

'Post-honeymoon jitters? Never heard of them.' Stephanos had said.

Sophia shot him a hard glare. 'Not surprising.'

'No,' Damon had said in a low voice. He drained the scotch and heaved himself to his feet. 'It's not that.'

He headed towards the door. 'Damon?' Sophia's voice stopped him. 'Is there anything we can do?'

He shook his head. 'I did it all myself.'

Kate had known it would be difficult. She hadn't expected to get over him just like that. But they hadn't been married very long. They hadn't even married for love. Surely those circumstances should dull the pain a bit?

The day she left Damon, she left the city, too. She didn't imagine he'd come after her, but if he had, she didn't know if she'd have had the strength to say no to him. So she fled, took herself off to New England.

Cape Cod in January seemed an appropriate place to go. A place as cold and bleak as her heart. Deserted, windswept miles of bare sand beach and chilly Atlantic surf were supposed to make her forget.

They reminded her of the Bahamas instead.

They reminded her of days in the sun, days of warmth, days in Damon's arms.

She lasted a week. Barely. Then she went home.

Only that didn't work either because her apartment, she discovered very quickly, wasn't home any more. Home was where Damon was.

As soon as she'd unpacked her bags, bought herself some groceries and spent a sleepless night remembering what it was like to share a bed with the man she loved, she took herself off to work.

Work had saved her from the pain of Bryce's defection and death.

It didn't save her from her love of Damon.

For three days she buried herself in interviews, home checks, the business of matchmaking families and nannies to help them. Nothing on earth helped her.

'You really ought to get some rest,' Greta, her office helper, told her late Thursday afternoon. 'That was supposed to be a vacation you took, but you look worse now than when you left.'

'I have a cold,' Kate lied.

'Then you should go home and drink orange juice and go to bed.'

But Kate shook her head. 'I have work to do.'

Greta reached over and plucked the file out of her hand. 'Then you'd better let me help you. You're putting the Barlowes under the Ms.'

She didn't fall apart while Greta was there. She waited until Greta caught the bus at five o'clock, then she stopped trying to pretend. Her occasional sniffles turned into honest sobs. She felt her heart rend.

There was a knock on the door.

Kate wiped her eyes, blew her nose, cleared her throat. 'We're closed. Come back tomorrow,' she said and her voice wobbled precariously.

'Kate? Is that you? Open up!'

She bolted up, wiping at her eyes even more furiously, hesitating, wondering if she should deny it, then going to the door. 'Stephanos?'

She opened it, still unsure. But, yes, it was. He looked frantic.

'Thank God!' He strode in, grabbing her by the arm.

'What's wrong? Is something wrong with Sophia? With the baby? Didn't Mrs Partridge — ?'

'Sophia's fine. The baby's fine. Mrs Partridge is a blessed saint.'

'Then what?'

He glowered at her. 'It's Damon.'

Kate's heart lurched. 'Damon? What's wrong with Damon?'

'You tell me.' Stephanos dropped his hold on her arm, but he didn't stop looking at her.

She shook her head, perplexed.

'He doesn't eat. He doesn't sleep. He doesn't shave. He doesn't work. Imagine, if you can, Damon not working! He does, however, drink. He drinks too damned much! And he looks like hell. And why? Because you left him, that's why!'

'I — ' Kate faltered, stunned.

'Why, Kate? Why did you leave him?'

She wet suddenly parched lips. 'Damon knows,' she said tonelessly after a moment. She looked away out the window into the darkness, unable to face her brother-in-law.

'That's what he said,' Stephanos admitted. 'But it doesn't make sense. You love each other!'

Kate didn't say anything. She couldn't deny it—not the part about her loving him.

And the other part? Wishful thinking, she told herself.

'You know, Kate,' Stephanos said carefully, 'marriages are tricky. They aren't long, smooth runs to perfect bliss. Seeing the hash I was about to make of mine should have showed you that. But you two had something real—the same as Sophia and I did.'

'We didn't!' Kate protested.

Stephanos just looked at her. 'Then why were you crying?' He nodded at the tissue still wadded in her hand. 'Why is Damon drinking himself sick?' He gave her a gentle smile. 'Take another look, Kate. Risk it. Go home. It worked for me.'

It wasn't the same.

She hadn't been playing around. And, despite what he'd said about fidelity during their brief marriage, she doubted that Damon would have cared if she had been.

At least that was what she tried to tell herself after Stephanos left her in the quiet of her office.

It didn't work.

Damon had proposed fidelity. He would have cared. He'd been honest about that.

But he'd never said he loved her.

And she'd never said she loved him.

She could—and did—argue both sides of the issue back and forth. And when she finished, she was no closer to resolution that when she'd begun.

She needed to talk to Damon to do that.

Could she?

Did she dare?

Wouldn't she be in danger of making an even bigger fool of herself than she had over Bryce?

She locked up the office and let herself out the main door onto the street. A brisk winter wind knifed through her, chilling her to the bone. She hurried to the corner and flagged a cab, eager to get home where it was warm.

But even in her apartment, she shivered. She forced down a bowl of soup, but it didn't thaw the cold.

Damon wasn't working. Damon wasn't eating. Damon wasn't sleeping.

Was he, she wondered, also cold?

She didn't know if she dared to hope. She suspected she might only be making her life worse. But in one way at least, she was her father's daughter: she was willing to take a risk.

She put her coat back on, knotted a scarf around her neck, and went back out into the cold.

There were no lights on in Damon's apartment that she could see from the street. Probably he was gone. Probably Stephanos had exaggerated. Probably she'd come in vain.

But she was here now. So she rode up in the lift, padded along the carpeted hallway, and let herself in.

The apartment was dark. Deserted. Damon must have given Mrs Vincent the night off. Kate stood just inside the door and wondered what to do now.

Actually she knew what she should do: leave. Damon wasn't here. Stephanos had been wrong.

She swallowed, turned, started to open the door to go out, then paused, drawn back by a need to touch one last time the place that had brought her closest to her heart's desire.

When she'd left him, she'd been in a hurry. Cold, but still desperate, needing only to get away.

And now—now she needed, if only in the silence of an empty apartment—to say goodbye.

She loosened the scarf, unbuttoned her coat, and slipped off her shoes, leaving them by the door. Then, with only the lights from the other buildings beyond the windows to guide her, she moved into the living-room. She walked slowly, trailing her hand along the back of the sofa, remembering when she and Damon had curled there together. She touched the bookcases, recalling titles she wished she'd read.

She moved on to the kitchen. There was a pile of dirty dishes in the sink. No sign at all that Mrs Vincent had been around. Had Damon fired her? It didn't seem likely. Still, from the look of things, for quite a while now he'd been on his own.

Kate picked up a coffee-mug from the counter, cupping it with her palms. She touched her lips to the rim where not long ago Damon's lips had been. Hastily she set the mug back down.

She paused at the door to the master bedroom. In the darkness she could see that the spread on the bed looked slightly rumpled. Otherwise the room lay untouched.

Slowly Kate entered. She walked around the bed, seeing in her memory the two of them lying there. Her throat tightened. Her eyes stung. Mindlessly she reached down and picked up a pillow, Damon's pillow, hugging it against her, pressing her face in the cool cotton, breathing in the scent of him.

Oh, God, it hurt!

She rubbed her face against it, furiously scrubbing away her tears and stalked out into the hall again.

'Who's there?'

The voice was hoarse. Ragged. Damon's.

Kate stopped dead.

She heard noises now, coming from the back bedroom. Then a silhouette appeared in the darkened doorway. A hand fumbled for the light switch then flicked it on.

'Damn it, Stephanos! Leave me alone. I — *you*!'

Kate's astonishment was just as great. Stephanos was right after all. Damon hadn't been shaving. Or eating, if the gauntness of his frame proved anything. Or sleeping, as the dark circles under his eyes pointed out.

'Damon,' she said quietly.

'What in hell do you want?' He glared at her through bloodshot eyes. He wore only a pair of undershorts and he braced himself by holding on to the doorjamb. He looked as if he might fall over.

'I — have you been sick?'

'I'm fine. I asked you a question. What're you doing here?'

'Stephanos said —— '

Damon said something in Greek about Stephanos. Kate didn't need a translator to know it wasn't complimentary. Then, right before her eyes, what little colour there was in his face seemed to wash right away. He turned and bolted for the bathroom. She could hear him being sick.

She wanted to go to him. She didn't dare. If she had any sense, she told herself, she'd leave. Damon certainly hadn't been happy to see her.

Still she stayed right where she was, waited outside the door while she heard the toilet flush, the tap turn on and, minutes later, off again. She took a step back only when the door opened once more.

Damon, still ashen and with damp dishevelled hair, stared at her. 'You're still here?'

'You are sick,' Kate said. 'You should be in bed.'

'I'll go to bed.' Damon's voice was a mixture of

weariness and irritation. 'Just get out of here.' He turned and headed back towards the small bedroom.

Kate followed him. 'Why aren't you sleeping in our —— ?' She stopped. *Our room*, she'd been going to say. She couldn't.

Damon shot her a malevolent look. 'Because I don't want to, all right?' He sagged onto the crumpled bedclothes and sat staring at his fingers which were laced together between his knees. He looked worse than she'd ever seen him. Defeated almost.

She had halted in the doorway. Now she ventured further in, only stopping when he lifted his eyes and scowled at her. 'Why don't you want to, Damon?'

His dark eyes glittered. 'What do you want, a pound of flesh? Christ, what did I ever do to you?' He jerked his head towards the door. 'Get out of here, Kate. Leave me alone.'

'You can't be left alone. You're sick. You need someone to take care of you.'

'Not you.'

The words slapped her across the face. She stepped back. 'All right,' she said. 'Not me. But what about your mother or one of your sisters?'

Damon snorted. 'No, thanks.'

'Eleni, then,' Kate snapped, goaded.

'Who?'

'*Who*?' She couldn't believe he'd said that. But he was looking at her, perplexed. 'Pandora's friend. The one who came to see the baby with her. You remember.'

He nodded, then rubbed a hand across his face. 'Why would I want her?'

'Maybe you wouldn't, I don't know,' Kate said, exasperated. 'But she's perfect for you. Lovely, talented, charming, maternal. Not to mention Greek.'

'So I should want her?' He still looked confused.

Then his gaze dropped and he bent his head so that once more he was staring at his hands. 'No.'

No? Kate, watching him, felt equally confused. Was Stephanos right then?

He had been about Damon's drinking, about his lack of sleep and food, about Damon's not working, about his looking like hell.

Was he right about him loving her, too?

Her fingers clenched. Her heart gave a tiny leap.

Damon glanced up at her, his lips thinning when he saw her still standing there. 'You don't have to hang around. I don't know what Stephanos told you, but ——'

'He told me that you love me.'

It was as if the world had suddenly gone still. Damon didn't move, didn't even breathe.

Neither did Kate. She waited. She prayed. She hoped.

At last Damon sighed, shut his eyes and fell back against the pillows. She saw his throat work. Then he opened his eyes and looked at her wryly.

'Does it say something about divine retribution, do you suppose, that I would marry you to keep him on the straight and narrow and he should be the one with the last laugh?'

'He wasn't laughing,' Kate said quietly. 'No one was laughing, because he also reminded me that I love you.'

Damon stared at her. He didn't speak. He levered himself halfway up so he was propped on his elbows as he searched her face. 'You love Bryce,' he corrected her hoarsely.

Kate pressed her lips together. 'Once I did,' she admitted. 'When I married him. He didn't love me.'

'But ——'

'He wanted what I had, the family fortune, exactly

what my father had predicted. And when Daddy cut me off, Bryce left me.'

'He died,' Damon protested.

'As he was leaving me.'

He shoved himself up off the bed and crossed the room, pulling her into his arms, holding her close. 'Oh, hell, Kate. I'm sorry. So damn sorry.'

Kate pressed against him, loving the warm strength of his arms around her. She rested her head against his shoulder. 'Thank you for caring.'

'I thought—I mean, all the time, when we made love——' He shook his head slightly as if he were dazed.

'You thought I was pretending you were Bryce?' She was astonished at his nod. 'Never. I never—it was never like that with Bryce.'

'It wasn't?' His voice was hoarse, his tone disbelieving.

She smiled. 'Not at all. It was barely tolerable. I. . .really didn't like it much. I thought I was frigid. So did Bryce,' she admitted shakily.

Damon snorted and hugged her tightly. 'Hardly frigid.'

She looked up at him, adoring him. 'Then I owe it all to you.'

'Why didn't you say?'

'Because it would have been changing the rules. We weren't supposed to care, remember?'

He pulled back and looked down into her eyes. His own were dark and still held a hint of desperation. 'I remember. It was hell. I wanted more. I thought you didn't. And when you took off for East Hampton, that confirmed it. It seemed that what mattered to you was your work.'

'I thought it was all I was going to have left.'

'No,' Damon said. 'Oh, no.' He kissed her then. It

was a deep kiss, a hungry kiss. 'Oh, God, Kate. I've missed you. I almost died when I came home and found your note. What did you mean, then, about not being able to live the lie any longer? I thought you meant the lie that was our marriage.'

She touched his lips with her own. 'I meant the lie that I didn't care when I did. For a while after we got back from the islands, I thought we might make it. And then. . .then it seemed to start falling apart. You went to Montreal, I went to the Hamptons, and things began slipping away. You got more distant. And Stephanos told me about Eleni.'

'What about her?'

'Just that everyone thought she would have been a good wife for you, except you were married to me.'

'Damn Stephanos,' Damon muttered.

'It wasn't his fault. He was right.'

'No one is a better wife for me than you,' Damon said fiercely. 'You're everything I ever wanted in a wife.'

'And you didn't even know it when you married me,' Kate teased gently.

He smiled. 'I didn't know *you* when I married you. But it didn't take long. You got under my skin. You became a part of me. I love you, Kate. When you left I thought I'd die.'

'I almost did,' Kate said, and it wasn't a lie. The essence of her being was so tied to Damon that she'd barely been able to survive without him.

'I found your calendar—the one where you were marking off the days. . .'

Kate nodded shakily. 'At first it was because I just wanted to get through them, like a kid waiting for summer vacation. And then——' she ducked her head '—then I didn't want it to end.' She buried her head against the strong wall of his chest. 'I love you, Damon,' she murmured.

She felt his lips touching her hair, her ear, her cheek. 'I love you, too,' he whispered and found her lips with his.

'Thank God for Stephanos,' she murmured after a long, long moment.

Damon rested his forehead against the top of her head. 'I guess we do owe him, don't we?' he said a little grimly.

'Yes. You ought to give him a holiday.'

Damon shook his head. 'On the contrary, I think the way to repay him is to give him more work. He's carried the whole business for the past week and a half and right now he's off closing the deal with Belliard. I think I'll have to make him CEO after all.'

She looked up at him. 'But what about you? Won't you miss it?'

'I won't have time to miss it. The company presidency is a bit more than a figurehead title.' He grinned at her, then gave her a wink. 'Besides, I have other plans.'

Kate cocked her head, smiling at him, loving him with all her heart. 'Oh, yes? Such as?'

He drew her against him and touched his lips to hers. 'Such as showing you over and over and over again how happy I am that you're my wife.'

Harlequin Romance ®

AVAILABLE IN OCTOBER—A BRAND-NEW COVER DESIGN FOR HARLEQUIN ROMANCE

Harlequin Romance has a fresh new eye-catching cover.

We're bringing you an exciting new cover design, but Harlequin Romance is still committed to bringing you warm and contemporary love stories that are sure to touch your heart!

See how we've changed and look for these fabulous stories with a brand-new look:

#3379 Brides for Brothers
by Debbie Macomber
#3380 The Best Man
by Shannon Waverly
#3381 Once Burned
by Margaret Way
#3382 Legally Binding
by Jessica Hart

Available in October, wherever Harlequin books are sold.

Harlequin Romance®—
Dare To Dream

OFFICIAL RULES

PRIZE SURPRISE SWEEPSTAKES 3448

NO PURCHASE OR OBLIGATION NECESSARY

Three Harlequin Reader Service 1995 shipments will contain respectively, coupons for entry into three different prize drawings, one for a Panasonic 31" wide-screen TV, another for a 5-piece Wedgwood china service for eight and the third for a Sharp ViewCam camcorder. To enter any drawing using an Entry Coupon, simply complete and mail according to directions.

There is no obligation to continue using the Reader Service to enter and be eligible for any prize drawing. You may also enter any drawing by hand printing the words "Prize Surprise," your name and address on a 3"x5" card and the name of the prize you wish that entry to be considered for (i.e., Panasonic wide-screen TV, Wedgwood china or Sharp ViewCam). Send your 3"x5" entries via first-class mail (limit: one per envelope) to: Prize Surprise Sweepstakes 3448, c/o the prize you wish that entry to be considered for, P.O. Box 1315, Buffalo, NY 14269-1315, USA or P.O. Box 610, Fort Erie, Ontario L2A 5X3, Canada.

To be eligible for the Panasonic wide-screen TV, entries must be received by 6/30/95; for the Wedgwood china, 8/30/95; and for the Sharp ViewCam, 10/30/95.

Winners will be determined in random drawings conducted under the supervision of D.L. Blair, Inc., an independent judging organization whose decisions are final, from among all eligible entries received for that drawing. Approximate prize values are as follows: Panasonic wide-screen TV ($1,800); Wedgwood china ($840) and Sharp ViewCam ($2,000). Sweepstakes open to residents of the U.S. (except Puerto Rico) and Canada, 18 years of age or older. Employees and immediate family members of Harlequin Enterprises, Ltd., D.L. Blair, Inc., their affiliates, subsidiaries and all other agencies, entities and persons connected with the use, marketing or conduct of this sweepstakes are not eligible. Odds of winning a prize are dependent upon the number of eligible entries received for that drawing. Prize drawing and winner notification for each drawing will occur no later than 15 days after deadline for entry eligibility for that drawing. Limit: one prize to an individual, family or organization. All applicable laws and regulations apply. Sweepstakes offer void wherever prohibited by law. Any litigation within the province of Quebec respecting the conduct and awarding of the prizes in this sweepstakes must be submitted to the Regies des loteries et Courses du Quebec. In order to win a prize, residents of Canada will be required to correctly answer a time-limited arithmetical skill-testing question. Value of prizes are in U.S. currency.

Winners will be obligated to sign and return an Affidavit of Eligibility within 30 days of notification. In the event of noncompliance within this time period, prize may not be awarded. If any prize or prize notification is returned as undeliverable, that prize will not be awarded. By acceptance of a prize, winner consents to use of his/her name, photograph or other likeness for purposes of advertising, trade and promotion on behalf of Harlequin Enterprises, Ltd., without further compensation, unless prohibited by law.

For the names of prizewinners (available after 12/31/95), send a self-addressed, stamped envelope to: Prize Surprise Sweepstakes 3448 Winners, P.O. Box 4200, Blair, NE 68009.

RPZ KAL